STONE WATER

barbara snow gilbert

FRONT STREET
Arden, North Carolina
1996

For Ira Jean
and with thanks to E.H.G. III

Library of Congress Cataloging in Publication Data
Gilbert, Barbara Snow, 1954—
Stone water / Barbara Snow Gilbert.
p.   cm.
Summary: Fifteen-year-old Grant confronts the difficult decision
of whether or not to cooperate with his grandfather's wish
that he not be placed on life-support systems.
ISBN 1-886910-11-1 (alk. paper)
[Grandfathers—Fiction. 2. Death—Fiction.
3. Assisted suicide—Fiction.]
I. Title.
PZ7.G3725St 1996
[Fic]—dc20   95-50378   CIP AC

STONE WATER

My friends, nothing lives long except the rocks.

Song of the Kit Fox, Cheyenne

PART ONE

1

The bridge was part of the jogging path through the park, and would have been Grant's shortest route home. But two years ago, three planks at the top of the arc had rotted out, victims of Oklahoma's baking summer heat, sub-zero wind chills, and alternating torrents and droughts.

Grant stood on the pedals of his dirt bike and eyed the approaching gap. He and Avery had measured their flying wheelies off other ramps and curbs. The jump was possible. But it was also possible to mangle both bones and steel.

Pedaling again, Grant slipped his backpack off his shoulders, then eased it onto the prickly yellow grass, unloading the extra weight. If he made the jump he would walk back for it. If he didn't, well ... Grant pictured the three fallen planks, lying broken at the bottom of the ten-foot gully.

He took three deep breaths. Ever since sixth grade he had been going the long way around. But now he was in eighth, and today felt good. Leaning forward into the long handlebars, freeing his weight from the back of the bike, he began to pump.

There was a jolt with the first uneven plank. He was going fast and it almost threw him.

Two pumps before the top was his last chance to ditch. He knew; he had skidded to a stop before and barely made it. He passed that point.

A fraction ahead of the gap, he stopped pumping. As the front tire lifted off, he leaned back and pulled the bike up with him.

For one long-short moment, Grant and the bike hung, suspended, against the blue September sky.

He threaded the bike into its slot. Funny, Grant thought, a bike rack for one kid and one bike. He knew families with five or six kids where bikes fell abandoned on their sides in heaps and nobody ever bothered to use a kickstand or buy a bike rack. But his mom had "the neat gene," as she called it, and so, the bike rack for one bike.

Actually, there were two bikes, the other a black mountain bike. It was embarrassing, a fancy alpine bike like that in Oklahoma. So it hung from hooks in the ceiling of the garage, stiff and lifeless. Still, other kids rode expensive bikes . . . But Grant's father had given it to him. The black mountain bike didn't count.

Grant fished into his backpack, feeling for the cool edges of the tin cup. It was an antique, a trail cup that his great-great-grandfather had kept tied to his belt loop in his range-riding days. Grant always kept it nestled in the bottom of his backpack, to hold loose change, arcade tokens, and his back-door key.

"Hey! I'm home! Anybody here?"

Not that he expected there to be. In the old days Vidella used to be here when he got home from school. She would call down to him from some upstairs room where she was forever vacuuming. Then she would fix him a snack and sit beside him at the table while he ate it. And that was fine, for then. But now he was older and Vidella usually caught the bus home before school was out.

Grant swung his backpack up onto the assigned peg. Tomorrow he'd try the jump with the pack.

The jump. He had to call Avery. Now!

But his stomach was tearing his insides out. He could make a sandwich in twenty-two seconds flat, Avery had timed him. Twenty-two seconds was the exact outside limit of how long the call could wait.

Cabinets slammed open and shut, and bread, peanut butter, honey, bananas, raisins, and chocolate chips appeared and disappeared. Tipping a milk carton on his way to the phone, he guzzled straight out of it. His mom would never know.

For the first time Grant noticed the red message light, winking silently at him. He supposed he should listen to it before he called Avery, just in case it was something important, but even the shortest delay was asking a lot.

Grant punched the button with the corner of the milk carton and stood, waiting for the endless rewinding, taking monster bites out of his sandwich.

"Grant, this is Mom. Listen, hon, I don't want to scare you or anything—"

Grant stopped chewing.

"—but I'm not at work."

This was unusual. Grant's mother was The Honorable Allison Taylor Hughes, Judge for the U.S. District Court for the Western District of Oklahoma. A big deal. A nominated-by-the-President-with-the-advice-and-consent-of-the-Senate big deal. His mom never left work for personal reasons—well, almost never. There was the time she delayed a hearing because of his piano recital and had her secretary tell the lawyers there was a scheduling conflict. But it had to be something *really* important.

"I'm at the hospital. It's Grandpa."

"Grandpa," Grant said under his breath, setting the milk carton down on the counter.

Grandpa was Grant's grandfather on his dad's side. The grandfather who had passed his own grandfather's trail cup on to Grant. He was the only grandparent Grant had left.

"Now, I don't want you to worry," his mother's voice went on, "but something has happened. The doctors aren't certain, they have to run some more tests, but it's serious. Dad's in Chicago, remember, so I came out to meet with the doctors. A nurse from the rest home rode in the ambulance with Grandpa. She says that when he goes back—which they hope will be soon—he will have another room. The Home is moving Grandpa into the Other Wing. You know, the wing Grandma was in."

He knew. The Other Wing. It had a name, something like "Skilled Personal Care Unit," but his family just called it the Other Wing.

"Now don't worry, hon—"

She had said that too many times.

"I want you to go ahead to swim practice. But I'll probably be a little—"

Grant punched the rewind button. Without waiting for the machine to get to the beginning of the tape, he pushed MESSAGES and his mother's voice screeched into the middle of the sentence.

"—is moving Grandpa into the Other Wing. You know, the wing Grandma was—"

Stop. He did not want to hear the rest of the message. Did not need to hear it.

Grant left the sandwich by the milk.

The wallpaper above the door that led up to the stairs was smudged from Grant banking an imaginary basketball off an imaginary backboard. He passed under the smudge without jumping.

Something was waiting for him at the top of the stairs, something from Grandpa. It had been waiting for him—for this moment—for two years.

Grant's room was on the third floor. The climb never bothered him, but today, suddenly, his legs felt like he had strapped on weights.

His room took up the entire floor. They thought it had been a ballroom, from back in the days when the kind of people who originally lived in this kind of house had that kind of room on their third floor. There was a circular half-window at either end, and a crystal chandelier. His mom said the chandelier looked ridiculous in a kid's room, but Grant had insisted that it stay.

Grant crossed to the roll-top desk under the back window.

The desk had been a gift from Grandpa. Before it became Grant's, it was in the long room of the ranch house, opposite the pebble stone fireplace. The ranch was the Rocking H, an hour west of town. From the time he was five, it was where Grant had spent his summers—just him and Grandpa and Dill, the hired hand who still lived in a trailer on the property. They took care of what stock was left by then, fished, and porch-sat in the evenings, rocking their chairs on the creaky, unpainted two-by-fours while Grandpa told stories.

Grandpa was full of stories, mostly attributed to Grandpa's grandfather—Chaps, they called him—the same great-great-grandfather whose trail cup Grant now had, the one who had homesteaded the Rocking H. There were stories of buffalo stampedes, pretty dance-hall girls, and run-ins with outlaws. Grant had always thought his own life a major yawn in comparison.

As he got older, though, he had begun to wonder. Was it really possible for one person to have so many adventures? How much was fact and how much was Grandpa's storytelling running away with him?

Grant polished the desk twice every year, once on his birthday and once on Grandpa's, so he wouldn't forget. Vidella had shown him how. Now, running his hand down the oiled, bumpy curves of the slats, Grant remembered when the desk had arrived.

It was the same day Grandpa moved into the

Home. Grant was twelve. He would never forget standing there, watching Dill nail over the ranch house door. Grandpa said the move was his idea, to be nearer Grandma. But Grant knew his parents were behind it. "He forgets to eat," he'd heard his mom saying to his dad. "And he's nearly caught the ranch house on fire, at least twice."

Later that day Grant was arranging his collection of cavalry figures along his windowsill when a truck loaded with Grandpa's old furniture pulled into the driveway. A few pieces his mother was keeping were taken off. But the biggest piece of all came down the ramp for him, specially tagged by Grandpa.

The movers almost had a heart attack getting the desk up the narrow back stairs to the third story—after the remodel, the wide, curving front stairs only went to the second floor. Grant remembered his mom saying it wasn't worth breaking a back over. But he had stood at the top of the stairs and cheered them on. As far as he was concerned, it *was* worth breaking a back over. Definitely.

Grant spun the old piano stool Grandpa had always used as a desk chair. He remembered spinning on the stool when he was little, twirling himself into dizzy oblivion until he fell, collapsing with laughter, to the ranch house floor.

Those were the days he and Grandpa played hide-and-seek with a stick of Juicy Fruit. Whenever Grant was coming over, Grandpa would hide a stick of gum in the desk. Grant would search all the tiny drawers and pigeonholes until he found it.

It had been sort of like a grown-up version of the game when Grant had found the envelope. Had Grandpa been thinking of the Juicy Fruit when he hid the envelope inside the desk that was going to his grandson?

Enough stalling.

Grant slid the roll-top back and jiggled the skeleton key into the lock in the ivory drawer set into the first shelf. He took out the familiar lumpy envelope and laid it on the green felt writing pad. Running his fingers around the edges—the paper fibers were starting to fray from this habit—he read the words scratched by Grandpa's fountain pen.

"Grant, Only open this if they ever put me in the Other Wing. Otherwise, leave it alone. Grandpa."

The envelope was closed with a red thread wound around a tab on the back. Grant had thought about opening it, lots of times. But in the end he had decided that if Grandpa trusted him with just the little wound string to keep the envelope closed, he would keep the envelope closed.

Grant had kept the subject closed, too. In the two years since he found the envelope, he had never asked any questions or brought the matter up. Grant figured it was Grandpa's place to do that, and Grandpa never had.

Of course it might never happen—Grandpa might never go to the Other Wing. And the note said the envelope was to be opened *only* in that event. Grant had wondered whether he could destroy the envelope, or keep it locked away, without ever looking inside. Now, that was one decision he would never have to make.

Grant studied the red thread. It was all that had stood between him and this mystery for two years. And now, on a Wednesday afternoon, only four Wednesdays into eighth grade, at 3:40 P.M., Grandpa wanted him to unwind it.

3:40! Grant's eyes went back to the clock. Swim team was at four, and his mom had said that he should go. He didn't know how he could float, much less swim, as heavy as his body felt. But he also knew that he couldn't open the envelope yet. After two years of waiting and wondering, it was too quick.

Grant locked the envelope away and jumped off the stool, leaving it turning behind him. Grabbing his Speedo and goggles, he took the stairs three at a time. He pulled his homework out of his backpack and stuffed his swim gear in.

Pedaling to swim practice as fast as he could, Grant wished he were at the hospital, in the middle of the emergency that was suddenly swirling around his family. He would hold Grandpa's hand, there in the bed, like adults do to comfort somebody who is sick even though they usually didn't touch that person at all. There would be hushed conversations with the doctors. He was old enough to be in on that. He wanted to be in on the excitement. Should he feel bad for thinking that?

But there was no way to get there, it was way too far to bike. Plus, his mom had said to go to swim practice. She hadn't mentioned he had a choice.

Pumping along on his bike, Grant tried to picture his grandfather. He would be lying in some neat white hospital bed just like the one Grandma used to lie in. Were his eyes open or closed? Was he asleep or awake?

I found it, Grandpa. A long time ago. Just like the Juicy Fruit. I thought you should know.

Maybe his message was like a prayer. Grant didn't know; he didn't pray. But he thought as he pedaled along that maybe this was how it was done, this talking to someone who wasn't there.

A gust of wind picked up and pushed Grant along, then blew past.

It was after ten o'clock that night when the automatic garage door rumbled open and his mother's Jeep pulled into the driveway. Grant stuck the still-unopened envelope into his American history book and climbed up onto the writing surface of the desk. He could just fit there cross-legged and see down into the yard below.

Her slender figure was tipped over with the weight of a big boxy briefcase she lugged with both hands. He wanted to help her with it but knew that by the time he could make it down she would be inside.

Downstairs, the briefcase scraped against the tile as she slid it into its cubbyhole under his backpack.

"Grraaannt?"

He liked the way she called his name, with highs and lows even in just one syllable. "Yeah, Mom," he yelled back.

"Honey?" Her voice bounced up the narrow stairwell. "Are you going to make me come all the way up there to talk? I'm beat."

"Coming," Grant yelled, skating in his socks across the wood floor, then tumbling down the stairs until he almost ran her over, standing at the bottom.

"So. I guess you got my message," she said, brushing a lock of auburn hair out of her eyes.

Grant nodded. "Is it bad?"

"Bad enough. Do you think I could have a hug?"

"Yeah, as long as you don't tell anybody." Grant put his arms around her. When he was little she would squeeze him hard and pick him up off the floor, kissing the top of his head, but now they were about the same size.

Unwrapping her arms, she smiled, but it was a tight smile, her lips pressed together so that the upper one was barely visible. "Don't worry, hon. It's going to be okay." She ran her fingers through the cowlick at the part of Grant's hair, brushing the bangs up and over and out of his eyes. "Come on. Sit with me while I get something to eat and I'll tell you about it."

Taking his place on his barstool at the island counter, Grant watched his mom line up her pumps beside her briefcase and hang the jacket to her suit. She looks different here, he thought, from how she looks at work.

He had seen her in her courtroom a few times. The first time he was shocked. The bailiff's voice had boomed out, "All rise," and the door behind the bench had opened. She had stepped out in a long black robe and seated herself in the chair that dwarfed her—her "throne," as she jokingly called it—while everyone waited. He remembered thinking she looked like Alice after she had eaten too much of the grow-small cake, in that room with the high ceilings and huge furniture. She certainly didn't look like his mother.

She looked better this way, in her stocking feet, clanking around in the drawer under the oven looking for the frying pan. Not that he wasn't proud of his mother and what she did for a living. He was. But this was how he preferred her, more in proportion, more his mom.

"Did you get any dinner?"

"Vidella's leftover chicken."

She nodded. "Thank goodness for Vidella."

A little *whoosh* sounded as she lit the stove. She pulled a carton of eggs out of the refrigerator and began cracking them into a stainless steel bowl. The sound of her tapping and then collapsing the shells filled the room.

Grant interrupted after the fourth egg. "Mom? Uh, Mom?"

She looked up, her hand poised over the edge of the bowl.

"Are you going to eat all those eggs?"

She counted the yolks swimming in the bowl. "Oh. You want some?"

"I could eat."

She opened another egg, then began to talk, with no prompting from Grant.

"The Home called about two o'clock. Said Grandpa had some kind of attack. They noticed yesterday he seemed disoriented—he almost fell once—but they didn't think much about it. Then today he started having trouble with his speech. By the time the staff got hold of me, he couldn't walk, couldn't talk. Nothing. They were already on their way to the E.R."

She cracked another egg. "Right away, of course, I called the law firm in Chicago where Dad's working this week. Had them interrupt his depo to take a message in to him."

Grant's father was a lawyer, too. The "Hughes" in Nash, Brakeman & Hughes, the biggest law firm in the state. Nash being deceased and Brakeman being retired, Hughes was the biggest of names in this biggest of firms.

"We talked. But there wasn't any way he could come home tonight. He'll be back in town Friday."

His mother had by now cracked all dozen eggs and began whipping them into a froth. She poured the mass of yellow goo into the hot pan. "Would you like some coffee? I'm going to make some."

Grant was surprised. His mother had never asked him if he wanted coffee before. He tried to sound offhand. "Sure, thanks."

His mom didn't seem to notice she had offered anything unusual. She turned on the cold water and began measuring grounds into the top of the coffeemaker.

"So," she continued, "I went out right away. And the short of it is, Grandpa is very sick. At first the doctors thought it could be any number of things. A blood clot on the brain, a brain tumor—"

A brain tumor! A brain tumor was what Grandma had. A slow-growing primary brain cancer that had taken its time, thirteen years, to kill her.

"—but the CAT scan confirmed a stroke. For now, there's no movement in his extremities. If there's no change, the hospital will probably keep him a day or two for observation, then release him back to the Home for long-term care. He's stable and he's resting quietly. That's about it."

"So, you're saying he can't move? He's like, para-lyzed?"

"Yes. Basically."

"Can he talk?"

She shook her head. "Sometimes he makes noises. Sort of gurgling noises down in his throat. Like maybe he's trying. But that's it."

"Mom?" She was stirring the eggs. "Mother? Is he going to die?"

This time she looked up, and their eyes locked. "He might, Grant." She sighed and went back to the eggs. "We'll know more after the tests."

Grant set out placemats and silverware. "You sure were gone forever. What took so long?"

"For one thing, the Home had someone waiting for Grandpa's old room. We needed to move all his things soon anyway, and I just thought I'd rather stay and get it done tonight, myself. I have a trial starting tomor-row and your father's no help with things like this, so there was no point in waiting."

16

Was there an edge in her voice? Well, after a day like today, why wouldn't there be? But Grant hadn't noticed it until she mentioned his father.

"And then I had meetings with doctors—or rather, I was waiting to have meetings with doctors—for most of the afternoon."

She brought over two plates of steaming scrambled eggs. Setting the one with the equivalent of ten eggs in front of Grant, she climbed onto the stool next to him.

"And there were papers to sign. Everyone was busy. I don't know . . . "

The rivulet of coffee slowed to an occasional drip. Grant unclipped two mugs from the cupholders under the cabinet. "When can I see him?" he asked.

"Well . . . how about Friday after school? Grandpa may be settled back at the Home by then. You don't have swim practice on Fridays, and Dad's flight gets in at four, so he should be back in plenty of time. I'll recess early and we can all go see him together. Okay?"

Grant poured coffee for both of them. His mom took it black, but he wasn't sure he could get his down that way. Turning his back to his mother, he poured a hefty slug of milk into his.

"Man, Friday after school seems like forever from now, Mom."

He sat back down and tried the coffee. Not bad.

"How about Plan B? You could excuse me from school in the morning," he said, raising his eyebrows and doing his best to put the puppy-dog look that he knew she loved into his begging black eyes.

She shook her head and stirred her coffee, though she had added nothing to it.

"Listen, Grant, Grandpa's stable. If there's any change the hospital will call and I'll take you right over. I promise. But really, you're going to have plenty of opportunities to visit Grandpa. I think he's going to be in the Other Wing for a while."

"Like Grandma, you mean."

Grant remembered his grandmother. Usually she had been in a bed, but not always. Sometimes she was in a Geri chair, short for geriatric—a wheelchair like a La-Z-Boy recliner with a clip-on tray. That way she didn't have to hold up her own head or be moved to eat or sleep. Asleep in her bed or her Geri chair was the only way Grant had ever known his grandmother.

"Like Grandma," Grant repeated. "That's what you're thinking, isn't it?"

His mother stirred her eggs around on her plate. "Probably, Grant. Probably that's what I'm thinking."

2

Friday evening, the first of what would be six soft chimes reverberated through the living room.

Grant, stretched out on one of the twin love seats, legs dangling over the end, slammed his fist into his baseball glove and ground it into the pocket. He remembered his dad telling him once, "Never arrive anywhere on time. A powerful man is always detained by something more important, whether he is or not." Then he had winked. Grant smacked his fist into the glove again as the last of the chimes faded away.

"That's it. Betcha Dad went straight back to his office from the airport." Grant sprung up and over the back of the couch. "I'm calling."

His mother, at the head of a dining room table that seated sixteen before any leaves were added, looked up at him, said nothing, and went back to the legal brief open in front of her. She had come home early, changed into a sweater and jeans, and now was working while they waited, with her big weekend purse slung over the back of the chair.

Grant stabbed the automatic-dial number for his

father's office.

"Nash, Brakeman & Hughes." The voice was low and soft, like a cat purring.

Grant spoke up crisply. "This is Grant Hughes. Is Mr. Hughes in, please?"

"I will connect you with his office, sir."

Grant looked at his mother and rolled his eyes. She shrugged and turned another page.

They knew the routine. The receptionist would never indicate whether Mr. Hughes was actually in or not, even if he had just walked in front of her with his overcoat on his arm on the way to the elevators. A caller had to pass several gatekeepers to get that kind of information.

Two voices later Grant got to one he recognized. "Evelyn here. Whatya want?"

Evelyn had been his dad's legal assistant for as long as Grant could remember. Her voice was loud and raspy and exactly fit her appearance: a steamship, because she chain-smoked and always wore a suit in various combinations of black and white. It was the kind of voice and appearance Nash, Brakeman & Hughes buried layers and layers away from the front desk. But she was the one who made William Henry Hughes's office work, and everyone knew it.

Grant smiled at the thought of her on the other end of the line. "Hi, Evelyn. My dad still there?"

"Left twelve and a half minutes ago." Her voice sounded as if it were booming out over a P.A. system. "Wondered about it at the time."

Grant's father normally never left work until at

least seven-thirty.

"Well, I don't guess Dad mentioned it, but my grandfather, his father, had a stroke—"

"Didn't mention it."

"Anyway, we were all supposed to go out and see him this afternoon. At five o'clock," Grant couldn't resist adding.

"Five o'clock? You gotta be joking."

"I know. Not in this lifetime."

"Listen, kid, your father's not physically capable of leaving work at five o'clock. You know that. Now don't take it personally, it's just not something he can do."

"Hey, I think I hear him now, Evelyn, thanks. I'll see ya."

As Grant hung up, his father, wearing sunglasses with tortoiseshell frames, poked his head through the front door and then stepped in. A slim briefcase was in one hand and a leather suit bag hung over his shoulder.

"So am I in the doghouse with you guys?" He smiled sheepishly. It was a smile toothpaste companies would pay millions for, and it started to melt Grant just a little, as always, but he steeled himself not to let it and said nothing.

His mother rose to greet his father, and they gave each other a quick peck on the lips.

Grant had a picture in his mind of a different way his parents used to kiss at the front door. There was a kiss, but not quite so quick. And his dad used to put the briefcase down. And once—from his hip-high van-

tage point it had happened right in front of his eyes—
Grant had seen his dad's hand slip down over his
mother's buttocks when his father pulled her to him.
Grant had looked up, curious to see her reaction. She
was laughing. She looked pretty.

His father extended his hand to Grant. Grant took
it and returned the firm handshake.

"Well, Son, have you been a leader today?"

It was his father's standard greeting. Grant hated
it. What was he supposed to say? And what was so
great about being a leader, anyway?

Grant looked him in the eye. "Have *you*?" He had
never taken this tone with his father before, at least
not openly. He liked it. It felt good.

His father continued looking him in the eye and
pumping his arm up and down. The handshake was
even firmer. "I hope so, Grant."

"Come on, you guys." His mother grabbed her
purse and shoved them out the door. "Let's go."

Belle, a large, cinnamon-colored woman, was at the
nurses' station when they came in. Grant couldn't
help but return her warm smile. She had nursed
Grandma, and she knew a lot about their family. There
were hugs and conversation about how much Grant
had grown, all the usual reunion stuff.

"You two go on ahead, I want to talk to Belle."
Grant's mother waved Grant and his father toward
Grandpa's new room. "He's right down that hall," she
said, pointing.

As if they didn't know.

Grant read the names beside the doors. Some he remembered from when they used to visit Grandma here. But she had died almost two years ago, not long after Grandpa moved into the Home. That was when they stopped coming down this hall. Grant thought back on all that had happened to him since that time. Sixth grade to eighth grade. Hair on his chest and under his arms. A new age bracket in swimming. During all that, these people had been lying here.

Grant's father disappeared into one of the doors. Taking up a position opposite, Grant slouched against the wall, his hands in his pockets, and let his eyes find the nameplate.

HENRY HUGHES. Henry was Grandpa's given name, but he had always gone by Hank. Grant was glad they had used Henry. Henry was nobody he knew.

Inside Grandpa's room, at the bedside, Grant's father had assumed a military "at ease" position, hands behind him, feet firmly planted. From where Grant stood, the scene was set off like a painting, the frame of the door serving as the frame of the picture: his father's broad back, the bed, Grandpa's stiff profile—not a portrait, just an arrangement of objects, a still life. Once, his father unclasped his hands and Grant thought he was going to reach for Grandpa. But he didn't.

"Good afternoon, Dad, it's William."

It was a voice Grant had heard him use on the phone with clients. Here it was all wrong, too full of confidence, too cheerful.

"How are you feeling today?"

What a stupid thing to say. Also, apparently, the only thing he had to say.

A nurse passed Grant and went in. Grant's father bobbed his forefinger twice in her direction, as if catching the eye of a waiter. They whispered, and then, with a nod of his head, his father motioned her to follow him into the hall.

Grant didn't want to be caught watching. Trying to look as if he had just caught up, he shouldered by his father and went in.

Grant put the rail down and bent over his grandfather's face. Everything was still, except for Grandpa's eyeballs moving under the lids. Maybe he was dreaming.

There was a picture, Grant had seen it propped on the ranch house mantle. Grandpa wore his black Stetson, pulled low on his forehead to keep out the sun, which flashed off his oval belt buckle. Grandma leaned into the curve of his arm, with a garden-grown rose pinned over her breast. Behind them were the swollen curves of a 1940s pickup. If Grandpa was dreaming, he was dreaming of them, like that.

Or maybe Grandpa was awake. Either way, Grant should touch him, take his hand, let Grandpa know he was here. Suddenly Grant knew why his father had not been able to do it.

Grant checked over his shoulder; he didn't want his father to see him do this. But his father was paying no attention, talking with the nurse in the hall. Pieces of their conversation drifted in to Grant. "Hasn't opened his eyes . . . is taking his food . . ." Grant turned off the sound.

Grant lifted Grandpa's hand and placed it in his own palm. It was a hand that had known real work, but now it was pale and limp. The contrast with Grant's hand—dirt under the nails, calluses from the strings of his guitar, a telephone number scribbled in blue ink—made Grant's stomach ache.

His mother's quick gait was coming down the hall. Grant folded Grandpa's hand back over his chest.

"All set." Grant's mother entered the room talking. "More tests on Monday at the hospital. The Home can take him there and wait."

She slung her big leather purse over the closet doorknob, paused to pat Grandpa's arm, then went to the dresser.

"You or Dad aren't going with him?" Grant asked.

His mother pulled out the top drawer and began to sort and refold the undershirts and socks. "Well, hon, I don't see how I can with a trial Monday morning. And your father"—she shut the drawer and moved down to the next one—"well, he says he can't."

She looked at Grant over her shoulder, continuing to fold. "Grandpa will be fine, Grant. He won't know if we're there with him or not."

Should she be saying those things in front of Grandpa? What if he was listening?

Grant looked back at his father, still behind him in the hall. The nurse was gone and he was talking into his pocket phone. Grant didn't think they would be staying much longer.

Bending down to his grandfather's ear, he whispered, low, so that his mother, with her back turned as she sorted the drawers, wouldn't hear.

"It's me, Grandpa. I haven't looked inside the envelope"—he tucked a wisp of white hair behind his grandfather's ear—"but I will. Whatever it is, I'm good for it." Grant traced an X over his chest. "Cross my heart."

Back home, Grant closed the door to his room, cutting off his father's "Goodnight, Son" from downstairs.

He unlocked the ivory drawer and set the envelope in front of him, as he had done so often before. But this time was different. This time he was going to open it.

Now he understood why he hadn't been able to do it before. It had been important to see Grandpa in the neat white bed—to see with his own eyes that the condition had been met. He had and it was and there was no more putting it off.

Grant unwound the thread. Two times around was all it took. He tipped the envelope and a cassette slipped into his palm.

From his handling of the package, he had expected this. He turned the tape over—an ordinary audio cassette tape, Sony, no other label—and laid it aside.

Reaching back inside, he pulled out the letter.

Something was scribbled on the back. "Milk, eggs, salt, taters, bacon, chops, Post Toasties." Grant smiled. It was Grandpa's version of the Food Pyramid— "Bacon 'n eggs on the bottom and just a little salt on top." And it was typical Grandpa, who had fifty years' worth of baling wire scraps in the barn. "Always use everythin' twice 'fore you save it."

Grant knew he was stalling.

There were two pages, filled with the familiar scratches and blotches of Grandpa's fountain pen. Grant held the letter to his face and breathed in. Leather saddles and fresh hay. It occurred to him that it should not be possible for smells to linger all this time, and he breathed in through the paper again. Whether it was the letter or his mind playing tricks he wasn't sure, but Grandpa was there.

Come on, Hughes. You can do this.

Slowly, because it was hard to decipher the crimped handwriting, Grant began to read.

To my grandson Grant:

The story on the tape is one of Grandpa Chaps's. Guess that won't surprise you none. But this might—it's one you never heard before. I know, you thought you'd heard them all, but you ain't. You ain't got enough lifetimes for that.

I spose the story is kind of a test—like in the fairy tales when the youngest prince answers the riddle or slays the dragon and wins the princess. But let me tell you now, there ain't nothin like a princess at the end of this one.

If you know what it means—the story, that is, and what I'm askin of you—then you're old enough for the job. If you don't, or won't, then you're not. I'm not talkin about your age in years here, Grant, which I figure you know. Age has got nothin to do with nothin.

Some might say I should not put you in this position, and I have thought a lot about that. I do not like to make things hard on you, Grant, and this is hard. But here's the thing: life is hard. I can't protect you from that.

The other thing is this: it's not the boy's story. I repeat, it's not the boy's story. That's all I got to say about that.

Guess I got one other reason for askin you. Put simple—there ain't nobody else. Grandma's too sick, bless her sweet heart, and hopefully she'll be gone by the time you read this. I wish she and I had talked about things before she got sick. But we didn't, and I don't think it's another person's place to decide, even a husband of fifty-two years and counting. So, here we are, stuck in the mud, her mostly. And I have learned.

As for your pa, well, he and I were never close—not underneath close like a saddle and blanket on a lathered-up horse, the way you and me are.

Not to mention the fact your pa wouldn't do what I'm askin. Trust me, I know. A while back I went to a lawyer joker I read about in the paper, about gettin your grandma and me an Alive Will. What I found out for my hundred bucks is, it's a bunch of mumbo-jumbo that wouldn't help your grandma a bit, and wouldn't do half the things I want for myself neither.

Anyways, yesterday your pa ran into that lawyer joker and found out I'd been checkin into things. He bout had kittens. Said he'd a tore up such a paper if his mother or father either one ever signed one. Said we'd both have all the help modern medicine could offer whether we wanted it or not. Sides which, he said, you had to be <u>competent</u> to make out such a thing. I turned blue at that one, but I held my tongue.

So, don't go lookin for no Alive Will. Even if I'd left one with you for the little good it does, the damn thing makes you get the doctors involved. The doctors would have got your pa in it and there you go. As for your ma, I like her very much. But she's not my blood kin. Plus, somethin like this, guess who she'd talk to right off?

Just do as best you can, Grant. It might be too hard, and if it is, don't worry. Things go on.

Now I know that if you are reading this I am already gone in all ways but one. Let me tell you this from that other side. I love you and I miss you and I need you now more than ever.

Goodnight, partner,

Grandpa

P.S. I read this over just now and I know it sounds a little touched in the head. But Grant, I ain't touched. Re-read it and you'll see. I'm as clear-minded about this as I've ever been about anythin in my life. I just did not want to spell things out too clear because if somebody found it, it could mean trouble for you.

P.P.S. Excuse all the palaver. I always was a long-winded yackety-yak, which I guess you know by now.

3

Grant lay on his back, the hard edges of the wooden planks cutting into his naked shoulder blades, and looked up past the leaves to the patches of blue. He and Avery had built the tree house—platform, really, rather than a tree house—from remnants of the detached garage that fell down behind Avery's house years ago.

Reaching up, Grant jerked the rope that dangled down between the branches, and listened for the sound of the bell in Avery's room. Avery lived on the street behind him, and their backyards backed up catty-cornered. They had rigged the bell when they were kids.

Avery appeared at his bedroom window, red hair sticking straight up, rubbing his eyes. They used to wake each other up at all hours, the earlier the better. Now it had to be something really important to justify a Saturday morning bell.

Threading his body through the window, wearing only stretched-out pajama bottoms that barely clung to his narrow hips, Avery climbed out onto the roof. He clambered down the adjacent tree, jogged across his yard, scaled the stockade fence where their backyards touched at the corner, and swung into the over-hanging branches.

"What's up?" Avery asked, stepping gingerly onto a wiggling plank. Over the years the boards had become slightly unsteady.

"Fix your hair, man, I can't talk to you looking like that!" Grant said in mock disgust.

Avery felt the top of his head and grinned. That was the good thing about Avery. He was always grinning. "Sorry, I thought the invitation said casual," he said, combing the spikes out of his hair.

"Good news, bad news?" Grant asked.

Avery leaned over the edge of the platform to spit. Both boys watched the sudsy wad free-fall to the ground, and land, still intact, to one side of a big root running out from the tree along the surface of the soil.

"Your side, you decide," Avery rhymed.

"Okay." Normally Grant would have told Avery sooner, but he had been preoccupied with the business about Grandpa. "Good news is"—Grant tried to deadpan but he couldn't keep a smile off his face—"I made the jump."

"All right, man!" Avery extended his palm and they high-fived. "I was afraid you were gonna miss your woo."

"My what?"

"Your woo. W-O-O. Window Of Opportunity."

"Oh yeah, right, my woo."

"You know. Like, for a long time, I thought maybe neither one of us was strong enough, brave enough, to make it."

Avery leaned back against one of the branches that grew up around the sides of the platform. Grant leaned back opposite him, counterbalancing his weight.

"And I thought," Avery continued, "one of these days, we're gonna be too big, too heavy, to have a chance. But you did it. You squeaked in there, Grant, right through that open woo. 'For one brief shining moment—'"

Avery started to sing the notes that went with the lyrics. He was a show-tunes junkie and knew all the words to every musical ever written.

"'—that was known as Cam-e-lot! Da da da *da* da-da-da-da *da* da-da-da-da, Cam-e-lot!'"

Grant was laughing. That was another good thing about Avery. He was *so* weird and he didn't even care.

"So now," Avery said, "the bad news. Hit me."

"Well, it's pretty bad," Grant said, looking up at the changing patterns the leaves made as they rustled in the wind.

"Get it out, Grant. Go. Do it."

"My grandpa. He's real sick." All of a sudden the breeze died. "They put him in the Other Wing."

Avery bolted straight up, causing the boards to joggle on his side. "And?"

Grant sat up too. "And? And he's sick."

"And . . . the envelope?" Avery asked.

"The envelope . . ."

"Yeah, for God's sake, man, the envelope. Did you open it?"

Grant pulled a sucker off one of the branches and

began twisting it in his fingers. "Yeah. I opened it."

"Go on . . ." Avery said, circling his hand as if he were reeling in a line.

"There's nothing to go on. It's a letter." Grant was doing his best to sound casual. "And a tape, another one of Grandpa's stories. That's all."

Avery was looking at him hard—Grant could feel it—but he kept his eyes on the thin green vine he was shredding. After a while he tossed it over the edge and lay back down flat. Avery matched his moves this time, and the boys lay alongside each other, knees bent so their legs didn't dangle.

"I can't say anything more about it than that, Avery," Grant said, turning his head toward his friend. "I haven't listened to the tape." Grandpa's letter had put him on guard.

They lay there in the silvery half-shade, dappled by the light coming in through the leaves. Finally, Avery turned his head and met Grant's eyes, only a few inches away. "Okay."

That was it. Not a problem. If he couldn't, he couldn't, no more discussion. That was the very best thing about Avery.

Grant had no idea how long he had slept, but the sun was higher behind the leaves. He felt rested for the first time in days.

"Hey, Ave," Grant said, elbowing him.

"Hey, Grantham." Avery, who could sleep anywhere, anytime, answered slowly, without opening his eyes.

"Wanna do the library thing?" Grant asked. He had tons of homework that he'd been putting off ever since Grandpa got sick. "My mom can drive us."

"The library thing? What's the library thing? Find a girl and make wild, passionate love behind the encyclopedias? I love you madly, madly—" Still on his back, hands clasped over his heart, Avery was suddenly singing, "Madam Librarian, Marian!—"

Music Man. That was the horrifying thing about Avery's habit—Grant was starting to know the tunes. "Put a cork in it, Avery."

"Let's see—library," Avery said. "That's the place with the books, right? Might go. But I don't have any homework to bring."

"Man, Avery, don't they ever give you any work at that school of yours?"

Avery went to school in an old red brick building in the heart of the city. Grant went to The Academy, a private school with a campus behind a wrought-iron gate. The two compared notes endlessly and had concluded that they traveled off to different planets between 8:15 and 3:15 every day.

"Homework," Avery mused. "Seems like I had some once. Couple of years ago, I think. Homework, yeah, that's what it was. But"—Avery paused for drama—"I got it done in study hall."

"Hilarious. Are you coming?"

"Well, there's one thing. My cousin Randi-short-for-Miranda is here—you remember, you've met her at my uncle's—anyway, she invited?"

Normally Grant would have said okay. But right

now his life was so complicated. He didn't want to deal with an extra. Much less an extra who was a girl.

"Come on, Ave, I've really got to get some work done."

"You're missing your woo here, Grant. She's excellent, I'm telling you, just your type."

"What's my type, Avery?"

"Totally humorless, now that I think about it. You're right, forget it, you wouldn't like her. She'd be way too much fun for you."

Grant shrugged. "Not today."

"Okay. Your loss, her gain. And if you can wait till after lunch, I'll go. Your woo will be gone by then."

All that day, Grant's thoughts kept returning to the tape shut away in the ivory drawer. In the end, what encouraged him was something Avery had said—all that jazz about being big enough, strong enough, having the right timing. And so, that night, after showering, washing his hair, and brushing his teeth—preparing himself—Grant took out the tape.

The sheets of his bed felt soft and dry against the lingering dampness of his skin. He fit the headphones snugly onto his ears so that Grandpa's dusty voice could whisper right into them, and propped himself at an angle against his headboard so he could see the star chart on the ceiling. He imagined himself small again, on Grandpa's lap, rocking, on the ranch house porch. It would be okay. Why had he been afraid?

Grant slipped the tape into the machine.

* * *

"It was the blizzard of '86. No Man's Land. Now it's the Oklahoma panhandle, but then it was nobody's.

"Grandpa—*my* grandpa, your great-great-grandpa Chaps—had been up the trail twenty years by then, and was winterin' longhorn before the summer drives to Dodge.

"This partic'lar day was so cold your piss froze fore it hit the snow. Grandpa Chaps was out workin' the herd—pokin' his fingers up their noses, pullin' the ice balls out so they wouldn't suffocate—when it starts to snow again. Lookin' up, he sees he's by hisself.

"He hollers for his partner, but there ain't no place that sound kin go 'cept straight off with the wind.

"Ever direction he looks, it's nothin' but gray. Couldn't tell where the horizon was. Couldn't a told up from down if he didn't know which direction his boots was.

"Decides the only thing to do is stay with the herd. 'Least wise I'll be movin',' he figures, 'and if I ain't found camp by night, I kin slit a cow and crawl inside her belly.'

"Well sir, pretty soon draggin' his feet is like draggin' two water buckets frozen to ice.

"Grandpa Chaps has his bowie knife pulled, lookin' for Old Blue—she was the biggest and too old for her own good anyways—when he runs plumb into somethin'. The stretched-out hide of a tepee.

"At first he figures it for abandoned, but he looks up, and sure 'nuff, there's a curl a smoke comin' out the top. 'Well,' he says to hisself, 'scalpin's sure as hell a lot quicker than freezin',' so he feels his way around to the flap and goes in.

"He squints, tryin' to see. It's the sorriest, starvinest bunch a Injuns you ever saw, huddled together in this one tepee, for warmth and to save their cow chips.

"His eyes are still adjustin' when he spots an old one lyin' next to the fire, wrapped up in the best buffalo hide. All sorts of feathers and beads and fancy things are settin' around his pallet, so Grandpa Chaps figures him for the chief and goes over.

"The chief's face is lined with deep cracks, so deep they look like they was carved with a knife, and his eyes are sunk in. Grandpa Chaps says, 'Howdy.' I mean, what else was he gonna say?

"The chief, he just keeps starin' into the flames and doesn't answer.

"But from behind Grandpa Chaps comes another voice, a girl-voice, and it says "Howdy" right back, just plain as kin be.

"He picks the one who said it outta the shadows. She's pretty, maybe fifteen, and she straightens her shoulders under the raggedy blanket she's holdin' around her and says in perfect English, 'We need to eat.'

"Well, she didn't need to say it for him to know it. Grandpa Chaps turns right around, goes back out into that blizzard, and butchers Old Blue.

"And that was the trade, shelter for food.

"They cooked the meat and ate it, and one of the old squaws, Grandpa Chaps figures prob'ly his wife, she chews up the meat for the old chief, then spits it out for him to eat, but he doesn't want it.

"There was one other that didn't eat neither. A tall one, with his long black hair loose, the medicine man. Even with the smell of that cookin' beef all around him, he didn't touch a bit of it.

"Well, they was holed up there like that for days 'n days. The girl's name was Bent Toe. She had learned herself English workin' in some army man's house at Fort Supply. She told Grandpa Chaps they was Cheyenne, Fox Band. And the sick man, she said, was a great chief named Wandering Shadow.

"Over the years Wandering Shadow had smoothed over a bushel a troubles 'tween their band and the white army. Like the time some a the young'ns stole the army's flag from the Fort. The army considered it a hostile act and was gonna move them to a reservation, which they was supposed to have done anyways. But Wandering Shadow went up to the Fort and told them, 'Did you never do something stupid when you was young?' and the army let it go.

"It was 'cause a Wandering Shadow they'd been left alone. An' now they were scared their chief would die, and leave them in these bad times.

"Well, the wind kept a-howlin' and the fire kept a-flickerin', and Grandpa Chaps and them Injuns just set around, suckin' the marrow outta them cow bones. All this time the medicine man, whose name Bent Toe says is Black Feather, is rattlin' and chantin' and smokin' up the tent. But no matter how fierce Black Feather goes at it, Wandering Shadow just lies by the fire, shiverin' and burnin' up with fever.

"Finally, late one night, they're 'bout crazy from the sound of that wind and those endless chants. Even Black Feather seems like he's all wrung out.

"That's when one of the boys, not yet a brave, but close, steps outta the shadows and squats down next to Black Feather. Eyes closed, holdin' perfectly still, the boy waits for Black Feather to speak to him.

"Accordin' to what Bent Toe told Grandpa Chaps, this is what they said.

"'What does Gentle Rain come to say?' Black Feather asks, finally recognizing the boy.

"'Gentle Rain comes to say that Black Feather doesn't need to call the Four Winds to help Wandering Shadow.'

"'How can a boy child know what will help Wandering Shadow, when all the magic of our grandfathers' grandfathers has not?'

"'Gentle Rain can help Wandering Shadow. But Fox Band must truly want it.'

"Black Feather says nothing. But after a while he turns over his place at Wandering Shadow's side.

"Picking up a dish, chipped at the edges, the boy reaches outside the flap of the tepee and scoops up some snow, then sets the dish close to the fire.

"He pulls the hides back from the floor of the tepee and scrapes at the frozen ground with his knife till he turns up a small stone. Then he takes a skin pouch he's been wearin' 'round his neck and pours out some dried berries. Poundin' the small stone against one of the bigger rocks that ring the fire, he crushes the berries into powder.

"By now the snow in the dish has melted and he stirs the powder into it. Finally he puts the stone in, centerin' it in the bottom.

"'Is Chief Wandering Shadow thirsty?' the boy asks, kneelin' beside the old man and raisin' his head. 'Gentle Rain brings Wandering Shadow's drink. If Wandering Shadow wishes it.'

"Wandering Shadow opens his eyes and looks into the dish with the stone and the water. After a long time he speaks. 'Nothing lives long except the rocks.'

"The boy nods. 'I bring you stone water. Hard as rocks.'

"Wandering Shadow's eyes, the whites yellow from the fever, move from the stone to the boy's face. 'Now,' he says to the boy. 'Now is a good time.'

"Then, with the boy holdin' the chipped dish to his lips, Wandering Shadow takes a long, long drink and lies back down.

"Gentle Rain sets the dish back on the fire ring. He takes off his skins and climbs into the hides with Wandering Shadow to keep him warm.

"That night it is quiet. No chantin'. Everyone sleepin'.

"In the mornin', Black Feather pulls the hide from Wandering Shadow's face and sees he is gone.

"'Gentle Rain's magic has sent Wandering Shadow away!' Black Feather shouts at the boy.

"'Black Feather's magic was keeping Wandering Shadow from going,' Gentle Rain answers, his head bowed.

"'The drink was poison!'

"'Water and berries.'

"'Berries! What kind of berries?' says the medicine man. 'You crazy boy child. Fox Band needed Wandering Shadow!'

"The boy looked up. 'Wandering Shadow needed to go.'

"'But Gentle Rain said he would help Wandering Shadow.' Black Feather's voice had changed. It no longer sounded angry. Now it was almost a wail.

"Gentle Rain picked the stone out of the dish, from which the rest of the water had evaporated during the night in the dry, smoky air, and tucked it into his pouch. 'Nothing lives long except the rocks.'

"And Black Feather said nothing more, because he knew Gentle Rain was right.

"Now Fox Band keened over Wandering Shadow's frozen body, still wrapped in the best buffalo hide, for two days. About that time the wind stopped howlin' and the sun came out. Grandpa Chaps took his bearin's from the Injuns and got ready to leave. But before he left, he told 'em, 'Take whatever you need from the herd, whenever you need it,' which he woulda got fired for had anybody ever known about it.

"Walkin' away, the sunshine blindin' his eyes where it bounced off the snow, Grandpa Chaps looked back over his shoulder at the tepee. He sees Fox Band—the women and young'ns too, like regular pallbearers—carryin' Wandering Shadow's body away.

"Well, Grandpa Chaps made the soddie in about an hour. He never saw that little scrap of tribe again, though he said he used to look for 'em every time he went through that country.

"Many, many years later though, when he was as old as I am now, he saw an obit in the paper. 'Bout a famous ol' Injun, loved and respected by his people, who had quietly lived out his days—always in a skin tepee, never a house—on his allotment from the Cheyenne-Arapaho Reservation, up on the north fork of the Canadian. A Chief Gentle Rain.

"Said he figured that boy had made a damn good chief."

The tape was silent. Grant, sitting straight up in bed, punched REWIND. He knew what he had heard, but he had to hear it again.

My God, Grandpa.

And Grant had told him, "Cross my heart." *Cross my heart and hope to die. Stick a needle in my eye.*

That would be easy compared to this.

4

October. Grant sat in American History, his next-to-last class of the day, looking out the window. On the other side of the glass the Bradford pear trees were slowly turning to flames. It was four weeks to the day since Grandpa got sick. A few days less since Grant read the letter and listened to the tape. *It was the blizzard of '86. No Man's Land.*

"Mr. Hughes!"

Grant jerked his head around to face Mr. Crowder, who loomed over him, slapping the length of a wooden pointer into the palm of his hand at Grant's eye level.

Grant gulped. "Yes, sir?"

"Mr. Hughes," Mr. Crowder continued in a knowing voice, "could you please comment on Miss Johnson's view?"

Grant looked down at his open history book, searching for clues. Out of the corner of his eye he could see Crowder's dark suit. The slap of the stick on flesh continued, as regular as a metronome. Should he bluff or be honest?

He looked up into the ice-blue eyes. "No, sir, I

couldn't comment on Miss Johnson's view. I have no idea what she said."

There was a ripple of laughter from the back row, but it died away sharply when Mr. Crowder looked up.

Grant had not meant to be funny or disrespectful, but maybe it had come out that way, he thought, confused.

The blue eyes were frozen on him. "For your information, Mr. Hughes, we were discussing the Boston Tea Party. Whether the rebellion was justified or not. Since we seem to have a little rebellion of our own at hand here, why don't you bring us a short paper on the question. Tomorrow."

Grant looked back down at his book, fixing his eyes on the print until the letters blurred and biting his lower lip. He could count on one hand the number of times he had ever in his whole life been in trouble at school, and he was not used to it. The tops of his ears were hot.

Crowder was a jerk. A throwback to the dark ages who made kids sit while he lectured about what was already in the book. Grant thought of a friend's boast that the only thing he had learned in Crowder's class was how to sleep with his head up and his eyes open—

The shrill bell cut off his thoughts.

Grant moved along in the swollen rivers of sixth, seventh, and eighth graders that poured into the locker-lined hall between classes. What would feel good was to slam all those lockers shut—no, kick them all shut—one at a time, down the row, as hard as he could. He was a good student, and Crowder knew it. Crowder shouldn't have embarrassed him. He hated Crowder.

Actually it was all Grandpa's fault. If he hadn't been thinking of Grandpa, he wouldn't be in trouble. Grandpa was ruining his life.

He remembered that night with the tape. After the third time through the story, he pushed STOP, took off the earphones, got out of bed, and locked the tape back up in the ivory drawer. Locked it *all* back up. Simple as that. Don't think about it. At all.

And it had worked. Until this afternoon, as he looked out the window. *If you know what it means— the story, that is, and what I'm askin of you—then you're old enough for the job.* He knew what it meant. Goddamn it.

Grant squeezed his way out of the main stream and over to his locker. When he opened the door, a bunch of his loose papers fell out. Squatting down among the forest of legs and feet, Grant retrieved them—already torn and printed with Nike tracks— and then elbowed his way back up and jammed the papers back into the locker.

Grandpa had no business putting him, a kid, in this position. He was trapped. As sure as if he had been crammed into one of the tight, dark lockers and the door slammed and locked.

He had to bust out. He had to see Grandpa.

Now.

The sound of air brakes drowned out the other traffic

as the bus lurched to a stop in front of him. Exhaust fumes spewed up from the underside, and the doors hinged open.

Grant cupped his hands and yelled from the curb. "You go to Sixty-third?"

The driver tipped his hat yes.

Grant had never been on a city bus. Taking a deep breath, which only succeeded in filling his lungs with fumes, he climbed onto the first steep step, offering more than what he figured to be enough cash. The doors swung shut and the bus jerked forward, pitching Grant into the first seat.

He had never cut class before. Considering this, the secretary who kept the attendance records might give him the benefit of the doubt. Maybe she'd think his mom had checked him out and somebody lost the slip. The worst that would happen—today, at least—was that the school would call home and leave a message checking up on him. Later, when it turned out he really was A.W.O.L., that's when there'd be fireworks.

Well, whatever the price, it'd be worth it. He was going crazy back there.

What was important was to beat his mother home. Not that he would erase the message from school, but he'd have a better chance of surviving this deal if his mother heard it from him first. Also, he didn't want her worrying. Worrying would put her in a bad mood. But he should be okay. His mom never got home until he was back from swim practice.

Swim practice. Man. And Coach. Man, oh, man. Grant hadn't thought about swimming. But the Home was sixty blocks away; there was no way he could be back in time.

Grant had never had an unexcused absence from swim team. From anything in his life, for that matter. Maybe he should call and leave a message at the pool for Coach. But what would he say? That he was visiting his grandfather? What kind of an excuse was that? Sounded made up. Wimpy. The truth had done him no good with Crowder, that was for sure. No, it was better just to skip.

Grant strained his eyes to read the numbers on the passing cross streets. Traffic was bad and the digits were rising too slowly, like mercury in a thermometer. He put his hand to his forehead and rubbed his temples.

Okay. Maybe cutting school and swim team and taking a bus clear across the city without telling anyone where he was going was a stupid thing to do. Maybe it would get him in tons of trouble. Maybe it would get him kicked off the team. Grant felt sick to his stomach. Maybe it was just the fumes.

Grant ran the three quick blocks to the Home, slowed to an acceptable pace in front of the receptionist, then jogged down the hall and into Grandpa's room. What he saw stopped him cold.

The bed was empty. The linens were turned back over the foot. Had Grandpa died?

Before Grant could think of other possible explanations, a dolly, with Grandpa on it, swiveled foot first into the room. A young man in a white jacket with a gold stud pierced through the side of his nose was at the head, steering.

Grant stepped up to the dolly and took Grandpa's hand.

"Family?" the man asked.

"Yes, sir."

There was a strong squeeze around Grant's hand when he said it, and he looked down at Grandpa, his heart suddenly pumping wildly in his chest. "Hey," Grant half shouted to the man, "he squeezed my hand!"

Grant had been here with his mom a couple of times in the last month. He hadn't wanted to come any more than that, it was too hard. Grandpa had always been totally unresponsive. Now he was getting better!

Maneuvering himself to stay alongside the dolly, Grant squeezed again, testing. The grip was returned, a secret communication. Was he ever glad he had come now. It had been the right decision, for sure.

Still holding firmly on to Grandpa's hand, Grant watched as the man stripped the old sheets off the bed and bundled them.

"Where did you take him?" Grant asked.

"Bath."

"Oh. That's good. I figured maybe he just got bed baths."

"We use the lift to give them a tub bath every week. Skin's so fragile it might tear if we tried more than that."

Tearing skin? Grant tried to imagine it and wished he hadn't.

"And once a month we give them a special Phisohex dip. He just got his first one."

Jeez. It sounded like dipping a dog for fleas. It would be Thanksgiving before his next one. Jeez again.

The man snapped open a clean sheet, which billowed out over the bed and filled the air with the faint scent of Clorox. Folding and tucking, he stretched the starched white sheet tight as he circled the bed. Vidella, their housekeeper, was good, but this guy put her to shame.

"Are you a nurse?" Grant asked. He had never heard of a male nurse, but hey, why not?

"Will be. Still in school. Work here in the afternoons. Name's Harland."

"Nice to meet you, Harland." What kind of a man would want to be a nurse? Maybe a really kind one. "I'm Grant. The grandson." The squeeze came again.

Finished with the bed, Harland came around to the dolly and folded the sheet off Grandpa's body, then began untying the strings of his hospital gown. Grandpa would have a conniption fit if he knew a man was taking his clothes off. For some reason it was even more embarrassing than a woman doing it. And what about Grant, should he leave? Turn around?

Before he could think any more about it, Harland whisked the gown away, as quick as a magician pulling a tablecloth.

Grant dropped Grandpa's hand. It was years since Grant had seen his grandfather naked, but this was not the body he remembered, stripped down for a quick swim in the red water of the cow pond. That body had been as strong as rope, with a bright tan line stopping at his elbows.

This flesh looked soft, sliding off the thin bones the way a water balloon filled with just a little water slides through your fingers. And there, in the center of the thin white fur, where his genitals should be, everything had slipped back, caught between his thighs so you couldn't see. Not even a man anymore.

Harland came up behind him and Grant stepped back, glad to turn over his place. In quick, graceful movements Harland slid a disposable diaper under Grandpa's hips, tabbed it up, threaded Grandpa's arms through a fresh gown, and tied it around his neck.

"Give me a hand?" he asked, turning to Grant. "Easier with two."

"Sure," Grant answered, still shocked by what he had seen and glad to hear he could speak.

Harland positioned Grant and they lifted him together. It was like lifting a rolled-up sleeping bag— bulky, but no weight.

"Thanks for the help," Harland said, already wheeling the dolly back out the door. "Thought, well, maybe he didn't have anybody, you know? Glad to see there's a nice kid like you to look after him."

Harland had forgotten the metal file folder he had been writing in.

It took a while before Grant was able to make sense of all the abbreviations, but he stayed with it. There were chronological records from the time of Grandpa's illness, reports from the initial hospital tests, and doctors' orders regarding medications. There was even a catalogue of telephone calls with lots of entries from "D-I-L." Daughter-in-law, his mom, he figured.

The section labeled Nurses' Notes recorded Grandpa's eating, sleeping, and even bowel habits. And there were comments like, "Pt" (patient, Grant guessed) "making gurgling noises from throat," or "constant REM." Rapid Eye Movement; he had learned about it in science. One entry read, "Pt firm handshake."

So. He had done it before. The handshake was nothing new, and it was not just for Grant.

At the end was a section labeled Prognosis. "Lng term deter expctd—No PT/SP recommd this time." Signed by doctor somebody. Reading it with some of the other comments, Grant finally hunched it out: no physical therapy or speech therapy recommended. They must think he was too far gone for it.

He let the metal folder bang shut. Nothing good in there, that was for sure. Thinking Grandpa would get better had been pure Disney. Time to grow up.

Grant wandered around the room. It was the first time since all this began a month ago that he had been alone with Grandpa. Now that he was, he didn't know what to do.

There was a new plant on the sill. The name on the card meant nothing. Some part of Grandpa's life Grant didn't know. Tucking the card in his pocket— his mother would want to send a thank-you note—he stepped on the pad of the stainless steel can to throw away the envelope.

The lid popped open and the sick odors of loose bowels and stale urine escaped. They were the smells Grant associated with his grandmother. They had been lurking there, in her room, all those years, and now they were here, too. He jerked his foot away and the lid flopped down, but not before he had seen the neat nest of diapers, bound into soft, round pouches.

Grant moved to the side of the bed.

Above the hat line from his Stetson, Grandpa's forehead was that of a much younger man. No spots, few wrinkles, lighter than the rest of his face by several shades. Below that, the skin was as tough as rawhide, cracked into diamond designs. Under the eyelids the eyeballs were constantly moving.

Grant sat down on the edge of the mattress.

He watched the rise and fall of his grandfather's chest. What would it look like if it were still?

Grant closed his eyes.

Down the hall a television was on. Outside, a dog barked.

What was it he had rushed here to say?

That it was too hard? How could he tell Grandpa it was too hard when he was the one lying in the bed, having his body cleaned by strangers?

That it was unfair? So what? So was waiting for a "dip" once a month.

He had come storming in here to tell Grandpa all the reasons why he couldn't do it. But really, what was there to say?

* * *

Uh-oh. His mother's Jeep was already in the garage.

As he came across the deck, Grant could see her on the phone in the kitchen. She turned and watched him through the French doors. There was a quick look of relief, then her eyebrows knitted again.

Big trouble.

". . . and tell Avery thanks again for going around the neighborhood."

Click.

She turned to Grant, hands on her hips, and sighed, blowing air up over her face so that it feathered her bangs. "Jesus, Grant."

His mother never said "Jesus." Never cursed at all, except maybe when she stubbed her toe or something, and then it was under her breath.

"Sorry, Mom." It was the only way he could think to start.

She put the palm of her hand out to him, like a cop stopping traffic. "Hold it. Before you say another word, I need to call your father. He made me promise to call him the minute you showed up."

Grant stood still, studying the pattern of the floor tiles, while she went through the necessary secretaries. "He's here, Bill, just walked in . . . don't know . . . I'll tell him." *Click.* "Your father says he will talk to you when he gets home."

Grant's insides sank. His father didn't often "talk" to him. He had really screwed up.

She pulled a chair out from the kitchen table and motioned him into it. "Take a seat, sir."

He had been sure he could soften the news from school if he could be here first to put his own spin on things. But he hadn't allowed for rush hour.

She had taken the seat opposite him and was waiting. "Well?"

"I went to see Grandpa."

He could tell she was surprised.

"I had to, Mom. Something came over me at school, and I *had* to go there. I thought I'd be back before you got home."

She didn't say anything for a moment. Possibly his sincerity had disarmed her. Honesty always did work best with his mother.

"How in the world did you get there?"

"The bus."

"The city bus?"

Grant nodded. What other bus was there? "I had to see him."

"That's not the point, Grant. No matter how badly you wanted to see Grandpa, it doesn't excuse skipping school. If you had called me at work I would have taken you—" She stopped.

Really, Mom? The first time I asked you to take me out of school to go see Grandpa, that very first day Grandpa got sick, remember, you made me wait two days.

"—probably."

Good. She remembered.

"We were worried sick about you, Grant. I got home early and there was a message from school saying you were absent last period and was there a miscommunication? I called the pool, even had them take a message in to Coach Roberts. He got on the line and said you had never shown up. I got scared and phoned your father, then made some more calls. None of your friends had seen you since Mr. Crowder's class.

"It was so unlike you, Grant. We thought something had happened."

"I should have left a note," Grant offered.

"You should have gone to class," she answered firmly.

Now it was Grant's turn to explain his side. His mother didn't interrupt, but without being able to tell her about the letter and the tape, Grant didn't think his urgent need to see Grandpa sounded very convincing.

"I'm sorry I worried you, Mom," he finished, "but I'm not sorry I went."

She got up from the table, crossed to the dishwasher, and began unloading the breakfast dishes.

"Mom?"

She turned her head, raised her eyebrows, and kept working.

"Grandpa squeezed my hand, Mom."

"Grant," she said to him over the clatter of the china. "I have tried to understand this sudden desire to see Grandpa. And I really do not understand it, although I can see that your need was real enough to you."

She quit stacking dishes and faced him, folding her arms. "Now, I am going to tell you something."

Grant remembered having thought that whatever the price of his actions, it would be worth it. Maybe he'd been wrong.

"Tomorrow I am going to call the school and take the blame for your unexcused absence. I will simply say, yes, there was a miscommunication about my checking you out."

Grant was stunned. He couldn't remember his mother ever saving him before. He got out a thank you, realizing that the words didn't begin to convey the relief and gratitude he felt.

"You're welcome, Grant. But it doesn't mean you didn't make a mistake." She unfolded her arms and put her hands on his shoulders. "Let's just say I'm giving you a do-over. Remember to give Dad and me one every now and then."

In grateful silence, Grant helped her put away the rest of the dishes. When the silverware was sorted, the cabinets organized and closed, he turned to her.

"I know this is terrible timing, Mom, but do you think . . . maybe . . . I could go back to the Home sometime? On my own." He paused. "It was good," he added softly.

"Not on school days, Grant." Her voice was normal—apparently she was done with the speeches. "And not evenings. I won't have you riding the bus alone at night."

"Saturdays. I could go Saturdays."

"You really want to spend your Saturdays at the Home?" she asked, sounding bewildered. "What would you do there?"

He shrugged. "Talk to him, be with him. Find out who sent flowers." As if to prove his point, Grant dug the card out of his jeans pocket and handed it to her.

"I'll talk to your father about it. Now go get cleaned up for dinner."

"The Boston Tea Party was justified because the colonists were protesting British taxes which violated the principles of democracy. As it turned out—"

A knock at the door interrupted the soft clack of the plastic keys on the computer keyboard, and Grant's fingers froze over them. It was his father's knock. It had that impatient rhythm.

"—the Tea Party was one of the events which led the twelve colonies to convene the First Continental Congress."

"Son?" His father's voice came through the door. He hadn't made it home for dinner, so Grant hadn't yet faced "the talk."

"Come in," Grant called back. "I guess," he added under his breath, continuing to type.

"The raiders acted for a higher purpose, and in spite of the danger that they might be arrested and jailed."

If he asks me if I was a leader today, I'll slug him.

His father was walking up behind him, reading the monitor over his shoulder.

"Breaking the law, in this case, was not a criminal act, but an act of courage."

"The Boston Tea Party," his father said. "Let's see. Trespass, breaking and entering, theft, destruction of property. I wonder what the merchants and farmers back in England who invested their life savings in that company's tea would say about your theory that those guys were heroes?"

He always took the opposite view. It was annoying.

Grant swung around on the piano stool and faced him. "Guess there's two sides to everything, Dad."

His father turned and started looking for a place to sit down. It was an act intended to break the tension—his father was backing off, starting over—but Grant made no move to clear the magazines and sweat clothes off his bed.

"Listen, Grant. Your mother told me that she's already given you enough speeches for one day." He hadn't found a place to sit, so he spoke standing. "And she's told me of her decision to call the school. I agree with it. A black mark like this would look bad on your record."

Hold it, thought Grant. That wasn't the reason his Mom was calling. She was calling as a simple act of charity. To say it was for a self-serving reason like protecting his record made it sound cheap and awful. But Grant didn't say any of that. There was no hope his father would understand.

"Now don't tell your mother this, but, man to man, Grant, I know why you did what you did."

Panic. Was it possible that his father somehow knew about the real reason for Grant's rush to Grandpa's bedside?

"Sure. Skipping school is a guy thing, I realize that." His father clapped him hard on the back, and the breath Grant hadn't known he'd been holding burst out. "I've skipped school once or twice myself.

58

A guy does it so he won't be seen as a goody-goody, so he can brag to his friends. I know that."

He seriously thought his son's cutting school and taking a bus across town to a rest home was about impressing friends? What planet was he from?

Bending toward Grant, his father lowered his voice. "Except, Grant, you made one mistake. You have to work the system, get your absence papered over."

Grant was listening carefully. He didn't want to miss a word of this laughable talk.

"Maybe, for instance, after an orthodontist appointment, you just don't come back. You were excused originally, so nothing sets off any alarms at school. I don't know, I don't know the system, but I know you're smart enough to work it.

"Be a good student, be a responsible kid, and don't try it very often." His father straightened and clapped him on the back again. "You can get away with a lot if people trust you."

Unbelievable. "The talk" consisted of coaching his kid on how to cut better.

"And as far as the bus trip goes, I think you showed a lot of pluck, getting yourself to Grandpa's and back by yourself."

Pluck? What a nerd word, it was too much. A smile overtook Grant's face and he spun around to hide it, pretending to go back to his paper.

But Grant didn't need to pretend. His father had seen the smile and was gone.

5

The team was swimming cool-down laps, twenty, at an easy pace. Through his goggles, Grant followed the lane lines under him, keeping his body evenly in between. The thick black stripes were his constant companions.

There were so many things Grant loved about swimming. One was the feel of his body cutting through the water, slicing one water molecule apart from the next.

Another was, he was good at it. Not great—not Olympic quality, not even the best on the city team— but good, one of three fourteen-year-olds who worked out with the fifteen and overs.

The pool was its own world. The seasons, temperature, time of day, all of it was irrelevant here. Even if something huge happened—say, if the president got shot—nothing here would change. Always the same watery colors, aqua and black. The same splash and thud of bodies stretching off the blocks and into the water. Even breathing the air—steamy and thick— was like breathing water, like you really were a fish.

And Grant loved the monotony. His fingers cut in

at the same angle every time. His legs pumped a steady beat-beat behind him. Even breathing was a pattern, not his decision. It freed his head for thinking.

Grant glided almost to the wall. Before touching, he tucked and flipped his legs over his head in a quick somersault, and pushed off. Taking full advantage of the glide, he restarted a gentle flutter, saving his arms until the last bit of momentum from the turn was gone. He reviewed what he had decided.

First, he would consider it. He wasn't saying yes, and he wasn't saying no. Just that he would think about it. He should make himself say what "it" was. Okay. He could.

Grant had learned lots of names for "it" from books in the library. "Euthanasia," a painless killing to end a painful or incurable disease. But what about the emotional pain? "Mercy killing." But "mercy" was something extended to a person, not something a person took upon themselves. "Mercy" sounded too much like pity, anyway, a word Grandpa wouldn't have stood for. And labeling it a "killing" weighted the argument against it; how could anybody be in favor of a "killing"? "Right to die" had the opposite problem—presuming something was a "right" made it hard to argue with. "Assisted suicide" was neutral. But "suicide" had too many bad connotations.

Grant rejected all the labels. For him, "it" was three simple words nobody had to look up: "it" was helping Grandpa die.

Flip. Turn. Splash. Push away.

Of course, if Grant were serious about even the

remotest possibility of helping his grandfather, he would have to force himself think about *how* he would do it. Otherwise he would not be ready, *if*. Grant had learned about some methods from his reading. But this was the hardest part to think about. Maybe he would never have to. Leave that one for later.

Tuck. Flip. Splash. Push away.

One thing he had decided: he couldn't tell anyone. He had considered telling his mother. Make her swear—like she made people swear, on the Bible—not to tell his dad. But she could never help him, even if she thought it was the right thing. It was illegal. And if he were caught there would be headlines, big, fat, black ones that would hurt her. She would have to be able to truthfully say she never knew.

Tuck. Flip. Splash. Push away.

And he wished he could tell Avery. Had come close, in fact, several times. But what if Avery told someone else? Felt that he had to? It could get out of control. And even if Grant didn't do anything and Grandpa just died in his sleep, if anyone knew what he had been asked to do, they would always wonder. No, Grandpa was right. Keep it a secret.

Tuck. Flip. Splash. Push away.

Needing to keep it a secret was why Grandpa hadn't bothered with a Living Will, the paper Grandpa called an "Alive Will" in his letter. Grant had learned about it from the books. A Living Will could tell the doctors to unhook a dying person from the machines, or sometimes to stop feeding them or giving them water. But Grandpa was right about that, too. In this family anyway, forget the public documents.

Tuck. Flip. Splash. Push away.

Regardless of the rest of it, there was one job Grant had right now. Grant had to take care of Grandpa— the others had deserted him. Had to be his family. Saturday mornings. If his parents would let him. They had to let him. He would open the blinds and let the sun in. Read to him. Turn the radio to the "Twenty-four Hours of Country" station Grandpa liked.

Tuck. Flip. Splash. Push away.

And Grant had decided one final thing: there was no rush. This was important. There was no reason to rush into anything. Grandpa would die on his own if Grant waited long enough. It was morbid, but it was true. He wished Grandpa would die. Today. This afternoon. It would be better for everyone.

Grant planted his arms on the side of the pool and pulled himself out in one quick, practiced motion. As he stood up, he popped his suit so that the excess water spilled out of it. It plastered itself back against the muscles of his abdomen and buttocks. Pulling his goggles down around his neck, he squinted, adjusting his eyes to the lights. The chlorine always put a glow around them, like a haze over the moon. Grant bent over and shook his head to the side in short, jerky movements until the suction broke and water trickled out from the ear below. He shook his head to the other side.

Practice was over and Coach had said nothing to him about missing yesterday's workout. He had almost stopped worrying about it. Until he heard the sharp chirp of Coach's whistle, bouncing off the tile walls. Still bent over and dreading the worst, Grant looked through his legs to see who it was for. He found Coach's eyes across the pool, fixed on him. He felt silly.

Slowly straightening, Grant turned and pointed to his chest, lifting his shoulders in a silent "Me?" Coach took the pencil from behind his ear and flicked it toward his office.

The office was a glassed-in cubicle from which Coach could keep his eye on the pool. There was no room for an extra chair, so Grant stood. The fifteen-and-over guys usually left him pretty much alone, but a few gave him sympathetic looks as they headed to the locker room.

There was a vent near the ceiling, blowing cold air. Wrapping his arms around his bare chest, Grant bounced up and down, shifting his weight from one foot to the other, trying to stay warm. Or maybe trying to calm his nerves, he wasn't sure which.

Coach was in no hurry, and Grant watched him check the ropes and measure chemicals into the pool. By the time Coach came into the office Grant was almost dry, and visibly shivering.

"Hughes!" Coach barked, banging his clipboard down on the desk. He was a short, strong stub of a man, wearing track shorts, canvas shoes, and a city team sweatshirt with the sleeves torn out and big white splotches on the front from the chlorine. Coach was not fun, but he was good. The team was the reigning state champion, and a number of graduating seniors always made it onto varsity college squads.

"Yes, sir!" Grant answered, focusing his eyes on the yellow pencil behind Coach's ear. It was sharp.

"Yesterday, Hughes. I seem to remember we had a practice yesterday."

"Yes, sir."

"Yesterday was Wednesday, wasn't it, Hughes?"

"Yes, sir."

"And Wednesdays we have practice, don't we, Hughes?"

"Yes, sir."

"Most Wednesdays or all Wednesdays, Hughes?"

"All Wednesdays, sir."

"Good. Glad to get that straight. See, one of my swimmers didn't show up yesterday and I thought maybe I was getting a little confused about it in my old age. Hughes!"

"Yes sir, I mean, no sir, sir!"

"Maybe it's none of my business, Hughes, but any reason why one of my swimmers might not have shown up at practice? Let's say a particular practice? Let's say yesterday's practice? Hughes?"

"I went to visit my grandfather, sir."

Grant sensed Coach looking at him, incredulous, but he kept his eyes on the yellow pencil.

"Any particular reason why you had to visit your grandfather yesterday, Hughes, between four and six o'clock?"

Maybe his voice was a shade softer. Or maybe Grant was just wanting it to be.

"Such as, an emergency, I hope?"

"No, sir."

"Such as, was your grandfather moving to Outer Mongolia this morning and it was your last chance to see him? Hughes?"

"No, sir."

"Anything, Hughes, tell me anything. I'm willing to listen. Be open-minded, even. If it was an emergency. Just give me something to work with here, Hughes."

"No emergency, sir. It was just a family matter."

"Any reason why this family matter wasn't an excused absence, Hughes? Why your parents didn't call in and excuse you from practice?"

"No, sir. Not really, sir. Possibly they could have, sir, if they had known I was going."

Coach was quiet for a moment, then looked down at the clipboard, reviewing the matrix of names, times, and events.

"Seems to me, Hughes, I talked to you about swimming the freestyle leg of the 400 medley relay in next week's meet. Bumping Fitzgerald and putting you in. You remember that conversation? Hughes?"

"Yes, sir." The other guys on that medley team were in high school. It was an open meet, which meant any age swam against any age, and it was the first time Grant had been offered a place on the older, faster squad.

"Seems to me, Hughes, that I really need a team player, for a relay, I mean. Wouldn't you say, Hughes?"

"Yes, sir."

"Seems to me I better swim Fitzgerald in that position after all."

"Yes, sir."

"Okay, Hughes, you're excused. Go get some clothes on."

Grant turned to leave, slipping and almost falling on the wet floor.

"And one more thing . . . Grant." Coach stopped him at the door. His voice *was* softer now. "This doesn't necessarily mean you did the wrong thing, going to see your grandfather. Maybe it was right, I don't know. I don't know the circumstances. But you have to realize, even good things can have bad consequences."

6

Saturday morning at ten o'clock, Grant rolled his bicycle off the elevator at the Brakeman, Nash & Hughes building. His parents hadn't said anything more about the bus trips to visit Grandpa, and Grant had figured he'd better not push it. In the meantime, they couldn't complain about him being here.

Evelyn had said to meet her on twenty-three. That was the floor dedicated to the firm's law library, sandwiched between three floors of offices above and three floors of offices below. Actually, Grant didn't figure he'd need much help. He was pretty good at libraries. Mainly he had just wanted somebody's permission to be here; his father was out of town, which was probably a good thing for once. No problem, Evelyn had said; if anybody asks, just tell them whose kid you are.

Grant had expected the library to be empty on a Saturday morning, so it surprised him when several people, all young, looked up as he rolled in his bike. Feeling *very* self-conscious, he pulled down the kickstand and sat in one of the leather chairs to wait for Evelyn.

Only after the heads bent back to their work did

Grant dare to look around at wall after wall of books, with sliding wooden ladders to reach them, and long tables with green-shaded bankers' lamps, sharpened pencils, and a fresh yellow legal pad set out at each place.

He pulled one of the books from the shelf behind him and flipped through it. Opinions. Were all these books full of opinions? How could there be this many different opinions about anything? And how did a person ever find the one opinion that agreed with their own? Maybe he'd been a little too cocky about not needing much help.

"Well, kid, I see you got yourself here."

Grant rolled the heavy book closed and looked up at Evelyn. These must be her casual, Saturday morning clothes—a knit pant suit, gray. She was branching out.

"What is it I'm supposed to help you with, anyway?" she asked, jamming her cigarette into the ashtray she carried with her.

"Well, it's an ethics paper, Evelyn. An ethics paper for my humanities class. On euthanasia—when sick or old people—"

"I know what it is."

"Right. Well, anyway, I've got to footnote the Oklahoma law. I know it might not sound like a very big deal, a footnote, but my teacher, man, she's in love with footnotes, it's like footnotes are her life, half your grade—"

"Get to the point, kid." Evelyn crossed her arms and looked at him over her reading glasses, which were slipping slowly down her nose. Some of the heads were up again, listening—smiling, Grant was pretty sure.

"Bottom line, I need to look up the Oklahoma law on assisted suicide, for the footnote."

It was the first time he had said words like "euthanasia" and "assisted suicide" out loud. It was also the first time he had told a real lie, an important lie. Neither had been as hard as he'd expected.

"Humphph," Evelyn snorted, her bosom bouncing. "It's gonna be a short footnote, I think. C'm'ere."

Grant followed her to a computer, where she punched in a search request. Together, silently, they read the short law.

"Every person guilty of aiding suicide is punishable by imprisonment in the penitentiary for not less than seven (7) years."

Evelyn exited and the monitor went to screensaver. "What I thought. It's a crime, not a defense."

"Uh . . . not a defense to what, exactly?"

"Not a defense to murder."

Grant cleared his throat. "Oh. I see. Well, in that case, maybe I should just look up, for the footnote, you know, the penalties for, uh . . . murder." God, murder was something—something awful, something evil—that a person did *to* somebody. Not something a person was asked to do, begged to do, *for* them. To *help*. How could the law not make some distinction?

From a shelf Evelyn pulled down two green leather books with Oklahoma Statutes, Criminal Procedure stamped in gold on the bindings. She slid them across the table and then turned away. "Look 'em up your-self. Your footnote-loving teacher wouldn't like it if I did all the work." From the door she yelled over her shoulder, "And reshelve!"

It took a while, but eventually Grant found what he was looking for.

"*A person commits murder in the first degree when he unlawfully and with malice aforethought causes the death of another human being.*" Grant's stomach turned over. He forced himself to keep reading. "*A person who is convicted of murder in the first degree shall be punished by death, by imprisonment for life without parole, or by imprisonment for life.*" His hands were sweaty; he wiped them on his shirttail and scanned the notes following the statute. "*In prosecution for first-degree murder, trial court properly instructed the jury not to consider sympathy.*" Enough already.

Of course, he was a juvenile. That might make a difference. He reshelved the books and looked around for someone to ask.

"Excuse me," he said to a young woman sitting behind approximately one hundred books and a six-pack of Mountain Dew cans.

"Yes?"

Man, she was pretty—couldn't have been more than twenty-five—wearing jeans and a tight sweater. He didn't know they made lawyers who looked like this. Maybe he would have to reconsider law school.

Grant gave her his own best smile. He had a good one, he knew. Time to find out if it worked on women other than his mom.

"I was doing research for a school paper, and I found what I need, but I have a question—a legal question—and I wondered if you could help me out."

"I'll try." She turned her chair to face him, pulling her bare feet up so she could sit cross-legged in the seat. She was wearing poppy-red toenail polish. His mind went blank. It was so, well, so *red*. "Shoot."

"Well . . . I was wondering . . ." He stretched the sentence out, looking down at the books in his hand and praying for a hint of what he was doing standing here—Yes! It came back to him. "I was wondering, if something was a crime in Oklahoma, but it was a *kid*, a *juvenile*, that committed it, would it make a difference?"

"It could. If a defendant's under eighteen, he might be tried in juvenile court."

"So a kid couldn't be sent to the penitentiary, or anything?"

"Well, sure he could. It depends on the crime. Take that murder rap I heard you talking to Evelyn about. On a charge like that, unless there's a special showing made to the court that the defendant should be tried as a juvenile, even a defendant just thirteen years old gets tried as an adult."

Grant nodded, not quite able to say thank you for that piece of information. "What if the same act makes you guilty of two crimes, say one with a less serious penalty and one with a more serious penalty. Which one do you get tried on?"

"It could be either. The D.A. decides."

Grant weakly smiled his thanks. "It's about what I figured."

"Sure. Whose kid are you, anyway?"

"William Hughes's. Know him?"

She laughed. "Who doesn't? Nice guy. Brilliant lawyer. Hope I get to try a case with him someday."

She reached for a fresh can of Mountain Dew, held it out to him, and when he declined, popped it for herself.

"Good luck with your footnotes. I had a teacher like that once. Gave extra points for every semicolon. I wrote a five-page paper, didn't use any periods—except one, of course, at the end. Otherwise all semicolons. Would have gotten an A too, but for one thing."

Grant waited for the punchline.

"She deducted ten points for every run-on clause."

Grant laughed. She was nice. He was starting to feel bad about all the lying.

The elevator fell fast, and his stomach came up in his throat. All the lies were just beginning. The whole thing, if he went through with it, would be one big lie. A silent lie. His grandfather would die and only Grant would know the reason and everyone would think it was something different and for the rest of his life Grant would have to let them think it.

The basketball thumped against the cracked cement pad where Avery's garage used to be, as Grant dribbled in place.

Avery's parents were watching the boys play from the porch swing—Grant had noticed Avery's mom's foot, wrapped like a vine around her husband's ankle. They were pushing themselves gently with their common leg.

This first Saturday had come and almost gone, and still his mother had said nothing about the proposed bus trips to the Home.

Grant dribbled and tried to catch his breath. "They're . . . *thump* . . . gonna say . . . *thump* . . . I'm too young . . . *thump* . . . I can feel . . . *thump* . . . it coming . . ."

Avery was hardly guarding him, probably wrung out from the one-on-one. "Too young . . . *thump* . . . to take a stupid . . . *thump* . . . bus ride?"

"That's what they're gonna say"—bounce pass—"you wait and see."

"Then the issue is"—Avery bounce-passed it back—"what do you say, to convince them they're wrong?"

Grant held the ball. "Here's what I say." He put up a hook shot that happened to go down. The ball bounced off by itself, then rolled into the weeds.

"I say . . ." Grant straightened his back, dropped his arms to his sides, and looked Avery in the eye. "I say, Grandpa's pa died when he was twelve. At thirteen he dropped out of school to run the ranch, so that his sisters could stay in school. At nineteen he rode tail gunner in the belly of a plane over Europe. A year later he got a hunk of his butt shot off and came home to marry Grandma and start a family. Too young? Too young for what?"

Grant quoted Grandpa's letter. "Age has got nothin to do with nothin."

The recognizable impatient knock sounded over the music. Grant closed the latest issue of *Sky & Telescope* and glanced at the clock just as the numerals rolled over to 12:00 midnight. Grant thought his father was still in Dallas. He must have taken the Red Eye back.

"Come in," Grant called.

His father looked weary. His tie was already loose, and he undid the first button of his shirt.

Maybe it was decision time on the bus trips. Grant turned off the CD player, reminding himself that it was in his best interest to be polite.

His father tossed his coat on the heap of dirty clothes covering the bed.

Grant, remembering the tense last visit, hopped off the piano stool and offered it, but his father waved him back on.

"This is perfect." He was already dragging an old bean bag chair out of the corner and across the floor. "I haven't sat in one of these in years."

Grant couldn't imagine him ever having sat in one, and wondered when he had.

He plopped down in the middle of the green vinyl bag, which poofed up around him. His knees were almost as high as his head. Ridiculous—a frog in the middle of a lily pad, all legs and joints. It was a new thing to see William Henry Hughes of Nash, Brakeman & Hughes looking ridiculous. Grant liked him that way. It made him different, somehow. Less a lawyer and more a dad.

"Maybe I should get a couple of these for the office," his dad said, patting the puffed-up sides. "My decorator could make me up one in a nice houndstooth or English plaid, don't you think?"

At first Grant thought he was serious, but now he saw from his father's tired smile that he was poking fun at himself. Maybe the humor was lame, but it struck Grant that his dad was actually trying here.

"Yeah, right, Dad." Grant settled on the piano stool and allowed himself to smile back. He hooked his legs around the base of the spindle and waited for his father's pronouncement on the bus trips.

But his dad was craning his neck to look around the room, taking in the telescope by the front window and the star chart on the ceiling.

Finally he spoke, in a far-off sounding voice, so that Grant couldn't tell if he was talking to him or to himself. "What happened to the rocking horse and the fire engine collection?"

Was he serious? He sounded serious.

After a while his eyes landed on Grant and he looked at him hard. Grant met his gaze, mentally rehearsing his speech and reminding himself to be respectful.

"Anyway, Grant," his dad said, shifting his weight and looking away, "what I came up here to tell you . . ."

Here it came. Maybe Grant should interrupt, jump in before the ruling was formally stated and set in concrete.

"Is . . . I'm . . . well, glad . . . "

Grant could hear the struggle in his father's voice,

and it surprised him. He had heard his dad argue law before the United States Supreme Court. He had watched him handle tricky media questions on live television. But he had never once seen his father nervous, or searching for words.

"What I'm trying to say is . . ."

What was this about? Not what he had thought.

His dad fished a folded cotton handkerchief out of his pants pocket and pressed it to his forehead. "I'm glad you and Grandpa are . . ." He smoothed the handkerchief along the ironed-in folds that Vidella had put there and tucked it away. "Close." He stopped. "I guess you might have noticed, but the two of us . . . Grandpa and I . . . well, we aren't. Close, I mean."

His dad looked up at him when he finished and Grant tried to mask his surprise, but he could feel his eyes widening in his face.

"Well, Dad, it's not exactly news to me."

Did it sound sarcastic? He didn't mean it to. He wished he could take it back. Maybe he had talked back to him so many times in his head that now, the one time his dad ever came to him and tried to have a real conversation, Grant didn't know how to. Quickly, making a conscious effort to change his voice, to *not* put him off, he added, "Did something happen? Between the two of you, I mean?"

Grant wondered if his dad would mention the fight over the Living Will.

His father shrugged. "We've had our differences."

So. Most likely there had been other fights, too

many to mention any particular one, and all just as bad.

"But did some *thing* happen? No, Grant. No *thing* happened. A thing doesn't have to happen for parents and children to drift apart. Sometimes it's just a habit . . . that happens . . . a habit of not being close."

A habit of working all the time, Grant thought.

His dad tipped his head back to the star chart. "All I ever wanted to do, Grant, was to help your grand-dad, you know. I saw him on his feet, his hands grimy, and manure under his nails so deep he could never get it out—"

Grant glanced down at his dad's own nails, buffed, with perfect half-moons just showing.

"—working all those years in that trashy old corral barn—"

Grant was shocked to hear his father thought it was trashy. He had thought it was wonderful. Full of dark corners and fresh hay, spider webs and barnyard kittens.

"—and all I ever wanted to do was help him. But he never could take anything from anybody."

Grant could remember Grandpa taking lots of things from him. Wildflowers. A turtle in a shoebox. Pictures he drew that Grandpa taped to the pebble stone fireplace. It was as if his grandfather were a puzzle and each of them had different pieces. His pieces were the grandson's pieces. He couldn't have his dad's pieces, and his dad couldn't have his.

His father was getting up from the bean bag, straightening his long limbs, changing back into his

78

original, towering self: the dad changing back into the lawyer.

"Well, believe it or not, Son, I've still got work to do tonight."

"Uh, Dad," Grant said, looking up at him, not wanting to let him go. "Grandpa's not that way with me, Dad . . . Grandpa asked me for help . . . once."

"That's nice, Grant," his father answered matter-of-factly, dusting his pants off as he spoke, a clear signal that it was time to wrap things up. "All I can say is, I hope you were quick about it. He must have been desperate."

His father hooked his finger under his coat and flung it over his shoulder, then flashed Grant his million-dollar, toothpaste-advertisement smile.

"And by the way, Son," he said from the door, "you can take the bus on Saturdays. Don't thank me, thank your mom." He started down the stairs. "I had nothing to do with it."

7

Grant sprawled on his parents' king-size bed. It was Friday night, and he could see his mother was going somewhere really fancy. A black cocktail dress was out of its plastic bag and hanging down the back of the closet door.

"What're the threads for?" he called into the adjoining bathroom, where she was putting on her makeup.

She stuck her head out through the doorway, her hair under a towel turban, her face washed clean.

"Annual meeting."

Grant knew this meant the yearly meeting of the Oklahoma Bar Association.

"Remember," she continued, "your father's president-elect this year."

Grant turned over on his back and punched on the television with the remote. "So where is Mr. President-elect, anyway?" he asked lightly.

"The usual. His runner came by for his tux an hour ago. He's going to meet me there. But I've got to be on time. I'm introducing one of the speakers at the dinner and we're sitting up front."

Grant was channel-cruising. There was nothing he particularly wanted to watch, but he left the TV tuned to the Discovery Channel, a program about volcanoes. He muted the sound and tossed the remote on the bed. "You know, Mom, you really don't need that junk you're putting on your face."

She bobbed out from behind the door again and smiled, a mascara brush in her hand. "Thanks, hon. What do you want?"

"Oh, man, give me a little credit," he said, grinning and putting his hands behind his head. "If I were trying to get something outta you, I wouldn't be that transparent."

Actually, he just thought she looked best with no makeup. Same for the girls at school. Between classes Grant stood with the other boys in a clump in the hall and watched them go in and out of the restroom door. He thought they looked better before they went in. He would never, ever be attracted to a girl who wore eyeliner. It was his solemn vow.

Leaning back against the headboard, Grant looked up at the ceiling fan turning lazily above the four-poster bed.

It would come from out of the blue, he knew, but when would it ever not? There was no transition for such a subject.

"Mom . . . do you think it's ever right to break the law . . . Mom?"

"What brought that up?" she answered from the bathroom.

"Oh, I dunno. Had to write a paper on the Boston

Tea Party, and Crowder gave me a B. Said I should have considered the other side."

"Which side did you take?"

"That it was right. To have broken the law."

"Well, I really don't know that much about the Boston Tea Party, Grant. But I would certainly agree that there have been lots of times when people have made courageous decisions to break the law. Think of the civil rights sit-ins. The Vietnam war protests."

"But were they *right*?" Grant asked, watching her through the door.

She slipped the towel off her head, shook out her hair, then plugged in the blow dryer.

"Mom, are you with me here, Mom?" Grant yelled, over the noise.

"I'm thinking," she yelled back.

After a few minutes she turned the dryer off and looked at him. "What's *right*, Grant? All anyone can do is try his or her best to think it through. It has to be a case-by-case, person-by-person, decision. Too many variables to generalize."

She came into the bedroom, took the dress off the hanger, and went into her dressing room. A few minutes later she was back, in the dress, stockings, and heels.

Something in her hand flashed; she held it out for him to see. Slithering through her fingers was a diamond and emerald necklace.

He whistled.

"I know" was all she said, dangling it out to him by the clasp.

"Where'd this come from?" Grant asked as he took it from her.

She sat down on the bed, holding her hair up from the back of her neck.

"He sent it over for tonight. Unbelievable, isn't it?"

Did she mean the necklace or the fact that his father had sent it to her? "No kidding" was all he said, slipping the clasp into its small gold catch. "Do you like it?" He watched her face in the mirror.

Her expression didn't change, but she ran her finger over the bumpy row of jewels circling her neck. "Do I like it, Grant? That's an odd question. Do I like it? It's elegant. If there's one thing your father has, it's perfect taste. Anyone would be happy to have it."

"But do you?"

"Do I what?"

"Like it."

She met his eyes in the mirror and her voice got quiet. "Well, I have it, don't I?"

"But do you like it?" Grant was whispering too; why, he wasn't sure.

"It's his way, Grant. Let's leave it at that." She got up off the bed. "You know he really is terribly generous." Her voice had its usual breeziness back.

Grant remembered his father's last birthday gift to him—expensive Rollerblades, knee pads, and a hockey stick left on the kitchen table. It was a nice gift, an extravagant gift, but he knew his dad hadn't been the one to pick the brands, check his size, or sign the card.

"He says Grandpa never would take anything from him."

"Well, that's the truth." Standing in front of the dresser mirror, she started to pin up her hair, section by section. "I remember once, Grant, this was before you were born. We were so worried about Grandpa and those steps up to the ranch house porch."

Grant thought of the loose steps with no backstops.

"Your father had the idea to have a railing put in. So when Grandpa took it upon himself to go visit Uncle Abraham that Christmas, I called a carpenter and had handrails built. I tied big ribbons around the posts and signed a card from your dad.

"Two days after your grandpa was back, I was over there helping with groceries, and the handrails were gone. Ripped out. Nobody ever said a word about it. Your grandpa is one stubborn old cuss, Grant."

So his mother had her own pieces of the puzzle. But Grant could understand why the handrails would upset Grandpa. The handrails were just like the Rollerblades; it was offensive for a person to take credit for a gift when someone else had gone to all the trouble.

But maybe there were other reasons the handrails made Grandpa mad. It was Grandpa's house; maybe they shouldn't have been messing with it without asking him.

Or maybe the handrails were like telling Grandpa he was old and feeble.

Or maybe they were right. Maybe Grandpa really just did not want to accept anything from his son.

Maybe he felt he had something to prove. Maybe the son had made him feel that way.

Grant realized that his mother was still talking, holding hairpins between her lips as she pinned up her hair.

"What?" Grant asked.

She took the hairpins out of her mouth and turned to him, hair up on the left, hanging down on the right. "What your grandfather doesn't know is, your father helps him every day."

"What do you mean?"

"I didn't want you to know when you were younger. I was afraid you might let something slip in front of Grandpa. But now you're old enough."

Grant waited while she pinned the last section up.

"Your grandfather's been living on Dad's money for a long time."

Grant bolted straight up in bed and flipped his legs onto the floor, facing his mother. "You're kidding. How could that be and Grandpa not know it?"

"Grandpa had invested in an expensive line of cattle he was trying to breed. Longhorns, actually, if you can believe that."

Grant could believe it. It sounded exactly like something Grandpa would do.

"Had some crazy idea about bringing the breed back, only as his new, improved version, making them commercial again. Only it didn't work. The president of the bank was a buddy of your dad's. He let your father know that the bank had already taken two mortgages and that they were going to have to foreclose unless your father did something fast.

"So your dad bought out the line. For a price *way*, trust me, *way*, over market value. Only Grandpa didn't know it was Dad, of course. Thought he had really made a killing on that deal."

She shook her head and went on to the next section of hair. "It was all done through our accountant. On the pretext that it was somebody else buying the stock. It's the money from that sale that Grandpa has been living off all these years."

Grant ran his fingers back through his hair. "Grandpa would be furious . . . " he said to the carpet.

But she heard. "You're right. Thank God he never got on to it."

Grant remembered Grandpa after Grandma's funeral. Grandpa followed the hearse in a taxicab—wouldn't even let them drive him—straight to the train station, where he supervised the loading of the coffin. He was taking Grandma's body back to Oregon. Her family was buried in some hillside cemetery, and there was a place for Grandpa there, too.

A picture of Grandpa's face behind the dusty little train window came into Grant's head. It was how he would look, now, if he knew this. Grandpa had sat stiffly, in his one suit and black Stetson, rapping on the window with his cane, telling Grant's parents, standing outside on the pavement, to go home.

Grant's father was steamed. He would buy a new family plot for his parents right there in Oklahoma. He would buy them a whole goddamn cemetery if it would keep Grandpa from making that ridiculous trip.

But Grant had understood. It was something Grandpa had to do. For Grandma and for himself. And he had to do it alone.

How would that man behind the dusty train window feel now, to know his ticket to carry his wife's body home had been paid for, not by him, but by William Henry Hughes? Grant thought of the Christmas gifts his grandfather picked out for him every year—the books with the handwritten inscriptions, the fishing pole, the restrung guitar. Grandpa's three o'clock Dr. Pepper that he used to buy from the machine at the Home. All of it courtesy of William Henry Hughes.

On the television screen the volcanoes were silently erupting.

"Spittin' mad," that's what he'd be. Grant could hear him spit the words out, his face turning red.

Finished with her hair, Grant's mother stood in front of the full-length mirror. The dress was backless, tight-fitting. She checked the view from each side. "Not too bad for forty-five, I guess."

Grant looked at her, glad to have something to take his mind off what he had just learned. She looked great, even with the makeup, he had to admit. "You'll knock their conservative old eyes out, Mom. The cat's meow."

"Grant, I may be old, but I'm not quite old enough to be the cat's meow."

"Okay, groovy."

"Actually, nobody ever used that word much."

"Cool?"

"Okay, cool," she said, and started to laugh.

"Speaking of okay, is it okay if I spend the night at Avery's?"

"See, you did want something. You've just been distracting me all this time."

"So, is it okay?"

"It's okay if you're invited."

"I'm invited. I'm always invited. And remember, I'm going to see Grandpa tomorrow. On the bus. By myself. This is your free public service announcement as to my whereabouts. Remember where you heard it."

She smiled and started out the door. "You coming or staying?" she asked, her glossy nails resting on the light switch.

"Think I'll finish the program," he said, punching the sound back up on the remote. "But Mom, I do have one more question for you."

"Okay, but make it fast. I'm late."

"What would you do if you're the judge, and the guy who broke the law comes before you, confesses what he did, and tells you his reason—"

"You're still on that?"

"—and you think it is a right thing, what he did, whatever it was. But it was against the law. A serious crime. What would you do?"

"Well, I know what I hope I'd have the courage to do."

"Let him off?" Grant volunteered, watching the volcanoes turn themselves inside out.

Her heels clicked down the hall. "Apply the law."

8

Grant dozed in his sleeping bag on the floor of Avery's room. Mockingbird songs drifted in through the open window.

Did the windows open at his own house? Probably painted shut, Grant thought fuzzily. In the fall his mother turned the thermostat from air conditioning to heat, in the spring she turned it back. Maybe that was the difference. Why the air was softer here.

He stretched inside the bag. Should he get up? Finish his dream? Go back to sleep? This is what it's like to be a cat . . .

Conversation floated up through the vents. Susan and Zach, Avery's mom and dad, were down in the kitchen.

Drifting in and out of sleep, or something close to it, Grant remembered the scene in the kitchen last night.

He had laughed so hard his stomach had cramped and his eyes had watered. What was it that got them going? Oh yeah, Avery's three-year-old sister, Star. "One, two, buckle my shoe . . ." And on and on until she finished the performance, holding out her plastic tray full of carrots and brown rice, ". . . nineteen, twenty, my bladder's empty!"

They had all—including Star, though she couldn't have known why—exploded in laughter.

Platter and *bladder* did sound alike, thought Grant now. The rising, uncontrollable hysterics of the night before began to overtake him and he laughed out loud, waking himself by another degree.

Avery stirred. Only the top of his head stuck out of the bag, like a carrot poking out of the ground with the rest of the long body hidden below.

Carrots. Zucchini. Sprouts and brown rice. The five of them dipping out of the big wok whatever concoction Avery's dad threw together from his garden. If that kind of food were served at Grant's house he would refuse to eat it. Here he wolfed it down. Another difference, besides the air—the food at Avery's tasted better.

He pictured Susan down there now, feeding Star, her long, prematurely gray hair hanging loose, straight down her back, instead of in her daytime braid. That was the only difference—ever. Otherwise, same face, same jeans.

His own mother went through lots of transformations in a single day. Grant had seen her adjust her looks by the slightest of degrees. Changing a pair of pearl earrings to hoops. An alligator watchband to gold. A briefcase to a purse.

The conversation in the kitchen had stopped now. Maybe Zach, who taught high school English, was grading papers. Grant had seen him spend lots of

Saturday mornings that way, camped at the kitchen table, patiently poring over his students' work, interrupting the grading to talk with whoever came in.

The rotary blade of the coffee grinder whirred, on and off, on and off, and the smell of coffee beans wafted up through the vents. From Avery's room you could always tell what was cooking.

And cold pizza. That was the other smell. Still in the box on the floor down by his feet. Actually, it smelled pretty good. Man, he was hungry. Hunger was a great thing.

On and off. It was like his dream. Memory. Whatever it was. On and off.

He tried to get it back—it was *so good*—and burrowed deeper into the downy darkness.

Like a spectator at a tennis match, Grant followed Belle's hand between the bowl of oatmeal and Grandpa's open mouth. He had come straight here from Avery's.

Creeping over the outside corner of Grandpa's lower lip, dribble started its slow path down his chin.

Belle let it go, as if she were testing her ability to whisk it off with the edge of the spoon at the exact last moment before it dropped onto the napkin clipped around his neck. So far she hadn't missed.

"Want to try?" Her voice was deep and rich. If she were a bell, it was not a tinkling, silver one. It was a big, old, cast-iron mission bell, with an aged, mellow ring.

He knew what to do, but did he want to do it?

Belle made the decision for him and handed the spoon across the bed, her white uniform straining at the seams as she stretched. Motioning Grant to take her place, she got heavily up out of the chair.

The seat was warm from her body. Grant mixed the oatmeal with the milk in the bottom to keep it runny, so gravity could help take it down.

"Belle," he asked, carrying the first spoonful over, "how do you know he's hungry?"

Belle walked around to the head of the bed, tipping a little from side to side with each step, then lifted Grandpa's shoulders and fluffed the pillows under his head to improve the angle for the cereal.

"Policy is, we feed them everything on the tray, if we can get it down them—and I always do."

"But . . . it's not like he ever *does* anything. Not like he needs the energy, I mean. I feel like I'm stuffing him." Literally. It was just like helping Vidella with the Thanksgiving turkey, loading spoonful after spoonful into an empty cavity.

Belle lumbered to the linen closet and took out an extra blanket. "Your granddaddy needs the food, Grant. Keeps him strong."

"Strong for what?"

"For fighting this thing. For getting well, of course." She sounded amazed that this wasn't obvious.

"Belle, how many patients on this wing do you know of that ever got well?"

"Now don't you go cross-examining me like you were your big-shot daddy. I'm telling you, a body

92

takes a certain number of calories just to keep going at all. For your heart to pump, your lungs to breathe. It's important."

Grant scraped a dribble off Grandpa's chin. It came off with one swipe, except for a bit that clung to the white stubbles. "Doesn't it depress you?"

She laughed, a deep rolling laugh. "Depression is a rich man's word, Grant. You're smart enough to know that. Besides, what's to be depressed?"

"This wing. Working here."

"Child, this is the Lord's work I'm doing, and I wouldn't trade the honor."

He watched her restretch the sheets, pulling the top one so tight it pressed his grandfather's feet open at an even wider angle.

"Well, I'm sure . . . but still . . . not very many of them have much to look forward to. If you get me."

"Now just who in the world do you think you are to say your granddaddy hasn't got much to look forward to?"

She sounded angry, but Grant knew it was just her way of making her point.

"Who are you to say your granddaddy here's not just *joyful* to feel these clean sheets under his tired old flesh. Or to have a sip of cool water. Or to hear the birds singing outside his window. This here life is sweet, child, not that I'm saying the next one isn't. I'm just saying, don't ever, never, think it's less'n it is."

She folded an extra blanket over Grandpa's feet, then went to the window and swished the drapes open. A gardener kept up the grounds and it was a pretty view, though she blocked most of it as she stood looking out.

"It might not sound like much to a young'n like you, but when you're old, lying in a bed, thinking it might all be over soon, it might be a lot."

Turning around, she faced Grant. "Might mean more to you then—to *him*"—she patted Grant's arm—"than either of you ever dreamed it would."

She moved on to the plants, checking the dampness, sticking her fingers into the potted earth. "Know how he mumbles in his sleep? How his eyes move under there? I think he's remembering." She smiled. "When he was with your grandmama. Or when he was with you."

Grant remembered thinking the same thing the first time he saw Grandpa's eyes moving under the lids.

"You ever have a really sweet dream, child, so sweet you couldn't bear to wake up?"

Grant, scraping one final spoonful from the sides of the bowl, didn't answer.

"Maybe that's exactly how your granddaddy here feels."

There was still Jell-O to go, which Grant didn't want to feed him—Grandpa didn't eat sweets. But he knew without asking that Belle would insist, so he started in on it.

"But . . . maybe it's not so great. Maybe he, they, any of them . . . maybe they'd just rather . . . not."

"We just don't get to choose, Grant. And that's the way it is. Pick your cards up and play them as best you can. You might want to turn them in for another hand. Might want to drop dead at the ball game, might want to die in your sleep lying next to your pretty wife. But you don't get to choose."

She carried the pitcher into the bathroom and turned on the water. Raising her voice loud enough to be heard, she kept talking, calling out to him, so that her words took on a different dimension, echoing in the bathroom, coming toward him from behind.

"It takes courage to accept what the good Lord sends you." She turned off the water. "A lot more courage in facing things than in whining around wishing they were something they aren't."

She watered the plants, then came over to him. "So." She put her hands on Grant's shoulders as he spooned in the last bit of Jell-O.

"I apologize for giving you such an earful, Grant. It's just how I feel about my job. 'I was hungry and you gave me food. I was thirsty and you gave me drink. I was sick and you looked after me.' Matthew 25:35. It's what I do."

9

The next day was Sunday and Grandpa's birthday—not that it was any different from any other day for Grandpa—and Grant was giving the desk its semi-annual cleaning.

He always started at the top, worked down the sides, then did the insides, the shelves and cubbies, and finally the slats. That was the way Vidella had shown him the first time, and that was the way he always did it.

He poured the rich liquid onto the middle of his father's old T-shirt, then stuck a corner of the rag in his mouth and climbed up, assuming his usual cross-legged position.

The oak was golden, as if the tree had caught and kept the sun inside of it as it grew. And the liquid gave it a soft sheen, so that it reflected the light from the window behind it. The grain was fluid stripes, the tree's annual growth rings. Occasionally they formed a gentle whirlpool—an eye, watching him. What had this tree endured to earn those rings?

A year endured for Grandpa, too, Grant thought, massaging the wood through the soft cloth.

When he visited Grandpa yesterday, Grant had left a coffee-table book, *Early Ranches of Oklahoma*, propped on the dresser. It had a page about the Rocking H, with a color picture of the front gate and a drawing of the brand. In the margin Grant had written, "Also known as the best place in the world for boys to spend their summers." Grant had bought the book a long time ago and had been saving it for Grandpa's birthday. Now Grandpa would never see it.

Grant started down the sides of the desk.

He knew that Grandpa would never see the book because Belle had explained Grandpa's charts to him. Grant had seen for himself the steady, unmistakable decline in Grandpa's vitals.

Which was sad, but okay. Okay because it meant things would run their course without Grant having to . . . do anything. One night, in his own private moment, Grandpa would slip quietly away in his sleep, the way Grandma finally had. It was a matter of weeks, maybe. A couple of months at the most.

So it wouldn't be years. Surely that was what Grandpa had been so afraid of. The years. So Grant had not let him down. Surely.

Of course, Grant could be wrong.

He came to the ivory drawer. He hesitated, then unlocked it and took out the letter and reread it. This time, one part jumped out at him.

"It's not the boy's story. I repeat, it's not the boy's story. That's all I got to say about that."

Grant locked the letter away and went back to the woodwork.

97

Well, sorry, Grandpa, but you are wrong there. You are wrong, because if there's one thing I know after all my reading and thinking and talking, it's this: it *is* the boy's story, Grandpa. Maybe not the letter, or the tape. Those are your stories. But now, *now*, Grandpa, we're in a different story. Not the story of how an old man hoped or planned to go. But the story of whether his grandson helps him or not. *That's* the story we are in now, Grandpa. I ought to know. I am the one stuck in it.

PART TWO

10

Grant pulled the last of his papers out of the shelves and cubbies. It was April, his fifteenth birthday, and he was cleaning out the desk again. It was fun, going through his old stuff.

Pretty much everything, whether it went into the keepers file or the alternative file—a big green yard bag he would carry down to the recycling bins behind the garage—had an A on it. Grant expected A's. He *assumed* A's. An A wasn't how he measured a keeper.

To prove it, Grant stacked the last paper he pulled out, the Boston Tea Party theme with a B from Crowder, on top of the keepers pile, then climbed up.

Man, it was tight. His knees banged on both sides. Maybe fifteen was too old to sit on the top of a desk anyway, he thought, climbing back down. To his surprise he found he could easily reach across the top from where he stood.

So. Another year for him.

It was supposed to be the best. Eighth graders were on the top. The biggest. The strongest. Next year would be high school and he'd be on the bottom again. But this year, man, he had looked forward to eighth grade since he was a preschooler hanging on the playground fence, gawking at the giant eighth graders moving in clumps, not lines, in and out of the middle school doors.

And it was almost over. What letter would he write with a Sharpie at the top of this year, like the grades at the top of the papers he had been sorting?

School. School was good. The work. The library. The teachers. Except Crowder. School was an A.

Social life. Well, Avery. And there were other guys he had fun with. He wasn't in the fast crowd, but he wasn't sure he wanted to be. And he wasn't a total loner. A group of guys played street hockey on Sunday afternoons at the church parking lot. And Friday nights he always had a friend to go with him to the high school games or the movies. Social life was a B.

Girls. Unfortunately, girls hadn't happened. Zero. Zilch. Zippo. Nada. He ate lunch with Tracy and Kenna sometimes, and they were nice, but that wasn't what he was talking about. Cecilia Clark and Beth Kenneborough had both asked him to the New Year's dance. He didn't "like"—as in "like like"—either of them, but he went with Cecilia because she asked him first and it seemed like the polite thing to do. But the night itself had been mostly, well, long. No, he didn't see how he could give himself any grade in the girls department. Skip girls.

Home. Tolerable. Mainly because his father was never there. Home was a C.

Looks. His looks were going to turn out average,

he figured. Tall. Shoulders getting broad. All that swimming, probably. His voice had pretty much stopped caving in on him. No zits. Yet. His Mom said his black eyes were to die for, but that was mom talk. She even liked his cowlick. Which he hated because it made his bangs spring up on one side and made his face lopsided. Looks were a C.

Sports. Swimming was good. Better than good. It wasn't a hero sport, and it would never make him popular, but he was solid and he liked it. His times were improving and he was a help to the team—two firsts at State in the 50 and 100 meter free, a second for his medley team, and two fourths in back and fly. And the older guys had loosened up with him, smacking him on the backs of his thighs with wet towels. Jeez, it smarted. It was great. Swimming was an A.

What did that make? Two A's, one B, two C's, and an Incomplete. Probably about a 3.0 average. But that was without averaging in Grandpa.

Things hadn't gone the way they were supposed to there. At first there was a decline—no more hand squeezes, vitals dropping off. But then, over the winter, Grandpa's graphs had gradually leveled off.

The lingering had started to weigh on Grant. Lingering was exactly what Grandpa had not wanted.

Two Saturdays ago, though, there were signs of change. Grant had become a proficient reader of the charts, and he immediately saw, with relief, that the slow descent had begun again.

Really, Grant had become proficient at everything having to do with Grandpa. Grant remembered the time he took his mom and she watched, open-mouthed, as he fed Grandpa, shaved him, swabbed his mouth out, put Vaseline on his lips with a Q-tip, took his temp, and fixed the sheets. So was it the business with Grandpa that had kept eighth grade from being an A year?

Grant turned the cloth to a clean spot and poured more liquid on, then started on the cubbies, being careful not to drip oil on the ivory drawer.

He kept it closed now. The drawer. No reason to open it.

He never got the letter or tape out. In the beginning he had. Read it over and over. Listened to the tape lots, too. Had been obsessed with it. With worry, actually, last fall. Now that he thought about it.

But it had tapered off. Sometimes it would surprise him, like that arcade game where you bop the heads of the prairie dogs when they pop up. He managed to keep it pretty well batted down.

Not that he didn't think about *Grandpa*. Not thinking about "the business" didn't mean he didn't think about *Grandpa*.

He still went to the Home every Saturday. He was on a first-name basis with the bus driver, and had only missed two Saturdays since that first one. The first was State, the second was skiing in Aspen over spring break. Otherwise, he was there.

In the beginning he just sat, holding Grandpa's hand, and worked on remembering. One Saturday he remembered Grandpa teaching him how to bait a hook and clean a fish. One Saturday he took his guitar and practiced the plucking patterns Grandpa had taught him.

At first it was hard, going back into his brain cells where it felt dusty and dark, like the unswept corners of the tack room. But the more he did it, the easier it was. He got to where he could remember whole scenes, smells, even little chunks of conversation.

But lately, he didn't do it that much. It was like he had remembered himself out. Now he took his homework or a book.

Grant rolled down the slats. The track was nice and smooth. He rubbed his way gently down.

No, he couldn't totally blame eighth grade's not living up to expectations on Grandpa. The business with Grandpa was huge, but even if it had never happened, this year would still have been not great. Maybe that was just what fourteen was like. Maybe it was impossible for fourteen to be an A year for anyone. Well, no, he could think of kids for whom it was an A. Or at least it seemed that way.

Beep. Beep. Beep.

3:05! When he woke up that morning, he had set the alarm.

So forget fourteen. Fifteen sounded *much* older than fourteen. Fifteen sounded like cars and high school and paying summer jobs. Fifteen was going to be great.

"Move it, Grant!" Avery hollered as he came up the stairs. "My Mom's bringing the car around. Let's go!"

Grant was going to spend the rest of his birthday

at Avery's uncle's, who lived on the edge of Okemah, a town about an hour east of the city. East was important. A fault ran through the middle of Oklahoma City—go west of it, toward the Rocking H, and you got flat, dry, west Texas; go east, and you got rolling green hills, Arkansas.

Avery's uncle's was definitely east, a white frame house on the top of a hill with a barn and horses and dogs and cats and lots of land. So pretty you could buy a picture postcard of it at the Okemah Chamber of Commerce office down on Main Street—Avery had sent him one once.

Grant and Avery crashed down the stairs.

"Whoa, guys!" Grant's mother called from the dining room. "Sounds like a stampede. I would like to see both of you live at least another fifteen."

The boys trotted past her, still trying to edge each other out.

"Please slow it down to a dead run."

"Bye, Mom, we're gone," Grant called as they spilled through the front door, then raced for the back seat of the battered Volkswagen.

Susan was behind the wheel. Zach, Avery's dad, was on the passenger side, his hair tied back in a ponytail. Folding their limbs down like card table legs, Grant and Avery fitted themselves into the back seat next to Star.

Grant's mother appeared on the front porch. "Remember, hon, I need you home by ten."

He scrunched up his nose in a silent gesture of protest for Avery's benefit.

"Your father will be home by then and he'll want to at least see you on your birthday."

Passing her the thumbs-up sign, Zach confirmed what had been worked out already. Susan jammed the gear shift with the broken-off knob into first, and the little car lurched around the driveway, leaving Grant's mom, waving, between two white columns.

Grant was so cramped he could barely move, but he managed to crank his window open and rest his elbow on the ledge. The day was cool, but the sun was strong enough to burn its way down through it, and he felt the exposed patch of skin on his arm slowly turning pink. It was the first warm sun of spring and it felt great.

He thought of yelling out the window—so that the wake of air that rushed by the side of the car would carry the news—*My name is Grantham William Hughes and today is my fifteenth birthday!*

But he didn't. Instead, with his knees up against the back of the driver's seat and Susan's long braid dangling down between, he sat quietly and watched the redbud trees pass by his window. The buds were swollen, ready to explode their red-violet color, as if a timer had been set and was about to go off. He knew just how they felt.

"Tck tck tck." Grant clicked his tongue against the roof of his mouth as he walked cautiously toward the bay, holding the rope halter up in his hands, ready to slip it around the horse's nose in the unlikely event he should get the chance.

The bay watched him from the side of his face, chewing grass with what seemed to Grant like a smirk on his lips. Grant took two careful paces forward, and the horse took the same number back.

They had traveled this way across the whole field and Grant was beginning to doubt he would ever catch him. Avery had caught his horse long ago and was lying back, his head on the horse's rump, his arm crooked over his face to block the sun, while his horse grazed, waiting for Grant. Their backpacks were packed with food and matches to build a fire, everything. But it all depended on Grant's catching the bay.

Holding out the halter, Grant approached again. "Tck tck tck tck." The horse backed off.

"Try letting him come to you," a voice said from behind him. A girl's voice.

It was a girl, all right. A girl with tied-back brown hair and light gray eyes. A girl with freckles across the bridge of her nose and a splash of sunburn under her eyes. An angular, long-legged girl, almost as tall as Grant, in jeans and cowboy boots. Grant was so surprised by her presence—and her looks—that his mind went blank. He stood staring at her, unable to think of anything to say.

"Let him come to you," she said again. She was concentrating on the horse, not him, Grant could see. "He has to think it's his idea."

Not sure what else to do, Grant looked back at the horse. Clearly the horse had the upper hand, and would not be caught if he did not want to be caught.

Grant lowered his arm so that the halter bent the

tall green grass over. "Okay, horse." It was easier to find words to say to the horse than it was to the girl. "Forget it. Whatever you do, horse, don't come. Please don't come."

The horse stopped chewing and stared at him. It was a stand-off.

"If you leave, he'll follow you all the way back."

Grant looked skeptically at her over his shoulder. The same horse that he had spent the last thirty minutes trying to get within arm's length of, and now she was saying he'd just follow him back? Well, hey, he certainly had nothing to lose. He turned around and started the long walk back to the barn. The girl fell in beside him.

After a few steps Grant checked over his shoulder. The horse was standing still, watching them walk away.

"Don't look back," she said, looking straight ahead.

Grant dared another glance, but more out of the corner of his eye this time, and more at the girl than at the horse. Did he know this person?

"Uh, excuse me," he finally began, wanting to end the silence, "but have we met?"

She smiled, still looking forward, and kept walking. "Yeah. About, oh, I'd say a half-dozen times."

Grant felt the tops of his ears turning red. He hoped she didn't notice, but then, she probably didn't, considering she wasn't looking at him. A half-dozen times? Who had he met out here even once before, not to mention a half-dozen times? Avery had three cousins who lived with his uncle, a girl and twin boys. They were little kids, so they ignored them mostly.

Grant could hear the horse's four-legged gait swishing up through the grass behind them.

"I'm Randi. Avery's cousin."

Grant felt his jaw go slack but he caught it before it fell open. This was Randi? Randi-short-for-Miranda-Avery's-girl-cousin Randi? Randi was a little kid. Eight or nine. Or had he lost track? Maybe twelve or thirteen. Well, he didn't know, but she was supposed to be a little kid. His ears were flaming now.

"Randi, my gosh, I'm sorry. I didn't recognize you. Obviously, I guess. I guess it's been a long time. Since I've seen you, I guess." Oh God, Grant, stop with the running off at the mouth. But if he stopped, there would be a gap. And he didn't want there to be a gap. So he kept going, and there were no gaps. "I guess maybe the last time or two I was out here, with Avery, I guess maybe you, you weren't around, I guess. Or something."

What did he have to do to stop talking? Clamp his hand over his mouth? He pressed his lips together to try to get them to stop moving.

"It's okay," she said. "I think maybe I was spending the night away last time, and the time before that, I don't know, maybe I was at camp. So it could have been a while."

How could he not have recognized this person? It was impossible. She must have looked different then. Because if she had looked anything like she looked now, he would have remembered it. Definitely. And why hadn't Avery told him about her? That she was like this. He'd kill him.

She was talking about the horse.

"His name is Snickers. Because he has this funny whinny, sounds like a snicker, you know—"

She turned over her shoulder and threw an amazingly accurate whinny out of her mouth toward the horse. Grant dared a quick look behind him and saw Snickers pick up his ears, then his pace.

"—and because of his coloring. Sort of like the candy bar—

Snickers had caught up to the sound of her voice, and now his head edged up to them.

"—and because he's sweet. Aren't you, boy?" She reached up and around the horse's head—which now bobbed gently up and down, like a rocking horse, between them—and pressed her cheek to the horse's.

"Good name," Grant said, "did you think of it?"

"Yeah. Me and my dad. He was my thirteenth-birthday present."

"That's a coincidence, well, sort of, because my birthday is today, actually." Oh, God, that was a stupid thing to say. What did her getting the horse for her birthday have to do with today being his?

"Really? Well, happy birthday, Grant. Would you like to ride him? That could be my present to you. Because he only lets people ride him if I say so."

She smiled at him again. She smiled a lot. He was starting to remember her now. She had always had that easy smile. But he thought maybe she used to have braces. And she was skinny and her knees were always bloody. Well, not anymore. She had asked him something. If he wanted to ride. Oh, yeah, riding. He'd forgotten all about riding.

"Yeah, sure, I'd like to ride him. I would have asked you before, but Ave's uncle, uh, your dad, just said to have my pick. I didn't know. That you were here. I mean, that he was yours. Anyway, riding'd be great."

As he said it, she reached down and took the halter out of his hand and slipped it quickly up over Snickers's nose. Her fingers brushed against his as she did it and Grant wondered if she noticed.

Suddenly Grant remembered Avery. Where was he? Boy, was he going to be surprised when he saw his cousin Randi. Or then again, maybe he wouldn't be. Maybe a person didn't really *see* another person when the other person was their cousin.

Grant put his hand up to shade his eyes, scanning the horizon. There was Avery, almost all the way across the pasture on the opposite side. He was perched on the white fence, and someone else was perched beside him, holding his horse by the lead. Grant squinted. Jeez, another girl. Where were they all coming from?

Grant listened to the branches snap and pop and breathed in the aroma of burning cedar.

He sat on the ground, leaning back against a log, and Randi sat next to him, close enough that her jean jacket touched his sweatshirt. Avery and Leigh Ann, Randi's friend, sat about a third of the way around the campfire. She was laughing over Avery's rendition of "Surrey with the Fringe on Top," complete with buggy-driving gestures. But Grant liked just sitting.

The four of them had ridden, doubled up on each of the two horses, along the creek that circled the hill. Rolling up their jeans, they had waded, collecting skipping stones until their feet turned blue in the icy water. Grant figured there was a cow pond or a lake somewhere, where they would skip the rocks. But Randi circled back to the pasture and taught them how to skip the stones across the flat, nibbled-down grass that the cows had just grazed. Then they built a fire in a clearing and roasted two packages of hot dogs.

After they got started, Randi had proved easy to talk to. Like him, she was in eighth grade, but she was younger because she had skipped first grade, whereas Grant had started late—his dad had held him back so he would be bigger for sports. She thought pep clubs and cheerleading were a waste of time, which was okay because she wasn't a joiner anyway. She told him she ran track, and he told her about swimming. They decided track and swimming had a lot in common.

When they rode, she had ridden behind, because she was lighter, and she had put her arms around Grant's waist. It was the first time a girl had put her arms around Grant, for any reason. Of course, he figured, she had to do it, to hold on—or did she? Her touch was so light, like she could have balanced all on her own. He wished he could touch her now, on purpose, so she would know he meant it, but he wasn't sure how to go about it.

Grant picked up a stick from the pile of wood they had gathered. There had been a lot of dead branches under the trees that had fallen during the winter from the weight of the wind and snow. Poking the stick into the flames, he broke up a big log, which disintegrated into glowing red and orange coals. Thousands of flecks of light soared up into the night. There was no wind, so they went straight up.

The lack of wind wasn't uncommon—even in Oklahoma, the wind usually took a rest after sunset. But thinking back on it, Grant couldn't remember there ever having been any wind that day. A gift from the gods for his birthday. For this perfect day.

Randi was snapping little twigs in her fingers and tossing them into the fire. He reached over and picked up her right hand, stilling the activity, and brought it over to him. He had never thought he could do a thing like that, and there he had just gone and done it without even thinking about it.

Her skin was soft. God, so soft. Softer than he had ever imagined skin could be. Turning it over in his, he saw that her palm was callused from the heavy chores and working with the horses. Hard and soft at the same time.

"You have a long life line," he said, tracing it lightly with the pad of his finger. He had seen an article on palm-reading in one of his magazines. Brother, talk about needing to see the future. If he had foreseen this use for that stupid article, he would have memorized it.

"Really?" Her body pressed against his as she leaned in to see.

"Look. See the way it runs across here, unbroken, and wraps clear up around your thumb."

"Well, you know, it's a thing I think about some-times . . . because of my mother."

It was a reference, Grant knew, to the fact that Randi's mother had died when she was little, shortly after the twins were born. He didn't know the details. A car wreck or something.

"You still miss her a lot, I guess."

"At night, mostly, when I go to bed. That's when I especially feel the rock."

"The rock?"

"Oh, it's just a way I have of thinking about it. It hurts, you know. Like walking around all day with a rock in your shoe. Every now and then you take your weight off it, do something else, and then, for a little while, you forget about it. But it's still there.

"Crazy thing is, I think I could take the rock out—or make it smaller at least—but I don't really want to. It feels good to miss her. Sort of like stretching a sore muscle after running. It hurts, but it's a good hurt."

Grant was quiet for a moment. "I'm going to miss my grandfather that way. Already do."

"He's sick?"

"In a rest home. I think he's going to die soon. We used to do a lot of stuff together. And since my parents always worked, he took care of me in the summers when I was little. Taught me to fish. Play guitar. Stuff."

She squeezed his hand. "You know, dying, it's a part of it." Tilting her head back she watched the sparks riding the air currents up into the sky. "I miss her. But you go on. And . . . there's all of . . . this."

He knew what she meant. The fire. The chill. Her sadness, her easy smile. Hard and soft. It all went together in some way that he did not want to analyze. He just wanted to sit here and watch the logs burn down and hold her hand. He felt like he had one of the glowing, flickering coals deep inside of him.

Grant switched his bread sandwich—a piece of bread between two pieces of bread—to the other hand, and hit the imaginary bank shot at the bottom of the stairs.

"The Home called again today, Bill."

It was his mother's voice, from around the corner in the den where he had left them talking.

Grant froze in the stairwell, straining his ears to hear over the soft background music his dad had put on. The clear, bell-like sounds of ice cubes dropping into his father's scotch glass traveled easily through the walls, but the words were harder to catch.

"Said you hadn't returned their calls," she continued.

True to their word, Avery's parents had gotten him back on time. When they drove up, his father's black Mercedes had been parked in the driveway, which meant he had made it in from the airport.

"Happy birthday, Son." His dad had met him at the door. "Have you been a leader today?"

Grant was in such a good mood it didn't even bother him. He had just smiled and returned his father's handshake. "Hope so, Dad."

Then there had been the presentation, the only

word Grant could think of for it. His father had taken him arm in arm into the den, and after some preliminary conversation about his schoolwork and swim team—kind of like the introductory remarks at an awards ceremony—he had called Grant over to his chair. Reaching into his briefcase, his father had pulled out a Nash, Brakeman & Hughes file folder and had actually stood up before opening it and handing the contents to Grant.

A check, made out to Grantham William Hughes, for "Ten thousand and no one hundredths dollars," was stapled to a sheet of firm memo paper. "To: Grant Hughes, From: William H. Hughes, Date: April 21, Re: Fifteenth birthday." A typewritten note explained that an appointment had been made for him with his father's stockbroker, and concluded, "Love, Dad." In the bottom corner were the initials "whh:es." William H. Hughes's dictation, Evelyn Stockwell's typing.

Well, okay, it was classic William Henry Hughes and he had flown all the way back from Dallas to give it to him and Grant wasn't going to let anything spoil this day. He had smiled, thanked his dad, said it sounded like a really interesting project and he appreciated his dad trusting him with the money and he was sure he would learn a lot. It was almost frightening how easily he could come up with stuff like that to say. Then, after what seemed like an appropriately polite amount of time, he had excused himself to fix his sandwich and go to bed.

He was on his way up to his room when he overheard them.

"I told Evelyn to call them back," his father answered his mother.

"This isn't a call Evelyn can make for you, Bill."

Grant took a bite of the sandwich—all three layers of bread were white and soft—and stood quietly mashing it between his teeth.

"Well, what do you want me to do? Hold up an entire outfit of lawyers and witnesses and secretaries while I trot out there to talk to a couple of nurses?"

"I frankly don't care what you do. I just want you to be the one to do it."

Grant gulped the doughy mass down his throat.

"They want to put him on the machines before it goes much further. I.V. for hydration and nutrition. Respirator if necessary. That's the message they wanted me to deliver to you and I've delivered it."

For a moment there was no answer, just the sound of ice tongs dropping into the bucket. Then, "Well, that's exactly what I want. Whatever they say. Would you please just leave a message with . . . what's her name . . . the nurse . . . the black or brown or red or whatever woman—"

"Belle."

"Yes, Belle, tell Belle that's exactly what I want and to go ahead."

"I will call Belle tomorrow—you remember Belle, I'm sure, the lovely woman with the rich ethnic heritage—yes, I will call Belle and leave a message." Her voice had the same controlled tone that Grant had heard her use pronouncing sentence on convicted criminals who stood before her with their heads down and their attorneys at their sides.

"I will call Belle and ask that she please not leave any more messages for you here. I will suggest in some polite but unmistakably clear way that, after all, you are so rarely home. I will give Belle—you remember Belle, I'm sure, the lovely woman who took care of your mother for thirteen years and takes care of your father now—yes, I will give Belle Evelyn's pager number, your car phone number, your fax number, and your private number at the office. I will suggest that in the future she might have better luck reaching you at work."

The background music clicked off.

"He's *your* father, Bill. *Your* responsibility. I'm out of the loop and I'm going to bed."

11

At last, the black void retreated ever so slightly, revealing the gray outlines of his telescope against the front bedroom window.

He found his mother on the screened-in porch, already dressed for work and sipping coffee, newspapers scattered around her on the wrought-iron table.

She looked up, surprise on her face. "What in the world are you doing up?"

He saw her eyes moving down his body, from his chest, past the ripped-out knee of his jeans, to his bare feet.

"You know, hon, all of a sudden, you look fifteen."

"I need to talk to you, Mom."

Grant sat down and she slid the geraniums aside, clearing the view between them.

Where were all those speeches he had spent the night rehearsing? He could see them, swimming around behind his eyes, typed on little strips of paper, like the fortunes in cookies, each piece of paper with a different bit of wisdom he was supposed to quote. But someone had thrown them into the air and there was no time to sort them out. He took a deep breath.

"You can't let them put Grandpa on the machines."

She folded her newspaper and waited for him to go on.

"I've been in this as much as anyone, from the beginning, and I should have some say in the decision. I feel strongly that they shouldn't put him on. He wouldn't want it. I'm sure."

"You realize, Grant, that if they don't put him on the machines, he will die. Soon."

"Yes. But he's gone already."

"They say there's a possibility that if they keep him alive, he might regain some of his speech. Some movement."

"Speech for what? What's he going to say? Movement for what? To hold his spoon? Listen, he's done it. It's over. He's had a family, been in love—"

Grant looked away when he said this, knowing that even to say it was to admit it was a possibility, to disclose something about himself.

"—gone to war, taught his grandson how to brand cattle and play the guitar. They aren't going to make him well enough to do those things again. Dying is a part of living, and now is Grandpa's time for dying. Don't let them take that away from him."

She was waiting. But that was all there was to say. None of it was what he had planned. That other speech was still up there, floating around on the scraps of paper. But this one had come out well. He had sounded strong and forceful. He had sounded like his father.

She took a sip of coffee. "You are an eloquent advocate, Grant. An advocate in the truest sense of the word, speaking for someone who cannot." She took another sip. "I don't necessarily disagree with anything you've said."

Relief flooded through him.

"But."

Oh.

"It's not my call. It's your father's. And I guess you heard me tell him that last night or you wouldn't be here right now worrying about this."

"So, are you saying you agree with me or not?"

"I'm saying that I am not the person you have to convince."

She had made her decision. To withdraw. It would accomplish nothing to beg; Grant had learned that long ago.

"So I'll talk to Dad. Is he upstairs?"

"Already on his way to Dallas. The Early Bird."

"Did he call the Home yet? To tell them what to do?"

"Not that I know of. But he could at any point. And you know, Grant, once they put him on those machines, well, they won't take him off."

Grant nodded. She was telling him to hurry. But he already knew it. The machines could mean years in limbo. Everything he had promised himself he would not let happen. And once Grandpa was on the machines, the other options, well, they would be gone, unthinkable. Grant would not be able to take Grandpa off the machines.

12

"Yeah?"

It shocked him when someone other than the hotel operator picked up. Over the last three days he had gotten used to the sound of the phone ringing in the empty room.

"Evelyn?"

"You're talking to me, aren't ya?"

"Evelyn, it's Grant. Is he there?"

"He's here." Then she added, "But he's busy."

"Evelyn, you gotta help me. I'm dyin' here." He could see the headmaster watching him through the glass. Grant had spent so many breaks on the pay phone in front of the office the last few days, they were starting to wonder what was up.

"I'm sorry, kid, but they're working on a response that's got to be faxed off in . . ."—Grant visualized her looking at her twenty-four-hour wristwatch—". . . thirteen minutes, to get it filed today in Oke City."

"Tell me what to do, Evelyn."

Silence. Then, "We'll be back in the office this afternoon. He usually takes a break to return calls at four bells. I could put you down for a CB then."

"Fine. Put me down. But not for a call back. For an appointment."

Silence again. Grant waited her out. This was the type of straightforwardness she understood. She would help him if she could.

At last she spoke. "Sixteen hundred. Sharp."

Grant studied himself in the rear-view mirror of the taxicab: white pinpoint button-down, navy blazer. Clothes he rarely wore, but which his mother made sure were always available. His mom said he had serious eyes. For the first time, he saw what she meant.

There was a Taco Bueno bag on the floor, and the odor of stale burritos and refried beans was making him nauseated. It wasn't far downtown and he could have walked, but it was a hot day and he didn't want to get all sweaty. And he *wasn't* going to roll the bike in again. Also, his mother had excused him from swim practice. He had learned a few things.

In an effort to stave off the sickness, he rolled down the window and stuck his nose out like a dog. It looked funny, but what was a little embarrassment compared to throwing up in the back seat of a taxicab?

The cab pulled up in front of Nash, Brakeman & Hughes Office Tower, a black marble building that swooped up into the air over Grant's head. Not sure how much to tip, Grant gave the driver a ten and told him to keep the change. Probably too much, sure sign of a rookie. In lieu of a nod, the driver wobbled a toothpick up and down in the space between his teeth, then screeched away.

At precisely four o'clock, the chrome elevator doors slid open in front of him, like curtains opening on a stage set. It was a big space, filled with groupings of leather couches and chairs. In the center was a curving granite counter with a receptionist behind it. Floor-to-ceiling windows and an aerial view of the city formed the backdrop. As he stood there taking it in, the doors started to close. Just in time, he stuck his foot out, caught the doors, and stepped in.

A glass plaque hung over the receptionist's desk, suspended from the ceiling by nearly invisible wires. At the top, "Nash, Brakeman & Hughes" was spelled out in bronze Helvetica letters, the same typeface that Grant recognized from the firm's letterhead. Underneath was column after column of names. Scanning the columns for his father's individual listing, Grant tripped on the thick edge of the oriental rug, lunged forward to retrieve his balance, and came up eye to eye with the receptionist. She looked like the women sketched in fashion advertisements: high cheekbones, glossy hair, eyebrows shaped like McDonald's arches.

"May I help you?"

He recognized the cat purr in her voice from over the phone.

"I'm Grant Hughes," he said, his voice sounding thin. He cleared his throat and started over. "I'm Grant Hughes. I have a four o'clock appointment to see my father, William Hughes."

She raised one arch. "Of course. Have a seat and I

will tell his secretary you are here." She pushed a button and purred something soft into the receiver while Grant made his way to one of the leather armchairs.

"Would you like something to drink while you wait? A Coke, perhaps?"

His hands felt very empty. It would be nice to have a prop. "Sure, thanks. A Coke would be great."

She punched another button and ordered someone to bring the Coke. Man, did even the receptionist have a secretary?

By 4:30 the Coke was long gone, and Grant was holding a glass of melting ice. It was freezing his hands, but there weren't any coasters and he wasn't sure what he was supposed to do with it.

He heard Evelyn's heavy gait on the wooden plank floors, steaming down the hall toward him.

"Hey, kid. How are ya?" Her voice boomed out before she came into view, and Grant jumped up as she wheeled around the corner.

She was wearing a black skirt, a black jacket, and a black and white polka dot scarf tied in an unfortunate bow at the neck. Grant smiled at the sight of her. He liked Evelyn.

"Come on," she said, turning on her rubber heel and marching back down the hall.

Grant fell in two paces behind. He was still carrying the glass of ice, not sure what to do with it, and trying to keep up. "Nice to see you, Evelyn."

"Nice to see you too, kid," she said without turning around.

She showed him into his father's corner office. "I'll tell him you're here."

"Thanks."

"Make yourself at home." She was already back out the door.

Yeah right, Grant thought, looking around. Not very homey. A huge antique writing table that his father used as a desk sat up on ball and claw legs. Grant eyed the eagle's talons gripping the soft, round flesh of the globes. Except for a crystal paperweight with nothing under it and a leather desk set, the table was clear. Behind it hung an abstract painting as big as the wall, filled with bold colors and brush strokes.

A family portrait was propped on the console behind the desk. Grant went around and picked it up. Him, his mom, and his dad, grouped in front of the fireplace, the corner of the Steinway just showing. They looked stiff, even in cashmere.

His father's voice was coming down the hall.

"—and have our objections to their new eve-of-trial exhibits hand-delivered by five o'clock today."

Grant set the portrait down and hurried back to one of the chairs facing the desk. His father came in with Evelyn following, taking notes on a legal pad. "And don't forget to include a tabbed set of our own exhibits for their use—Son! What a nice surprise." He clapped his hands on Grant's shoulders as he passed behind, going around to his own chair. "Always glad to have you down here. And be sure we have a set ready for His Honor too—"

He hung up his jacket and loosened the noose

around his neck as he talked. "My God, Grant, you look like a lawyer yourself already. Fortune 500 material, wouldn't you say, Evelyn?"

Evelyn looked at him over her reading glasses. She passed out of the door as a secretary came in, an inch of pink telephone slips in her fist, which she handed across the desk to Grant's father.

"The only really important ones are on top. Senator Boone and John Wiggins. Would you like me to get them back?"

"Buzz me when you do—you don't mind if I take a couple of calls while we visit, do you, Grant?"

Grant was ready to say no, sure, whatever, but his father didn't stop for an answer.

"And get Lisa up here if she has a minute. She can do me while we talk."

The secretary pulled the door closed behind her and Grant was left facing his father across the desk. He suddenly remembered the glass of ice in his hands and realized his fingers were numb. Sticking the glass between his knees, he rubbed his hands on his khakis, trying to get some feeling back into his fingers.

His father leaned back in his chair, hands behind his head, the powerful artwork framing him from behind.

"Well, Son, have you been a leader today?"

"Uh, actually, Dad, in a way, that's sort of what I came down here to talk to you about."

"Really?" His father sounded surprised and pleased.

"Well, some decisions."

"Planning that run for freshman class president already? Or thinking about a summer job?" He popped forward in his chair and leaned over the desk toward Grant. "You know, Son, I could get you a summer internship up here. Filing court papers, running deliveries downtown. Helping out in the copy room and library. There's nothing like understanding a business from the bottom up. Wish I'd had that kind of opportunity when I was—"

A soft *mmm mmm mmm* interrupted him. Even the phones sounded luxuriant.

His father pushed one of the dozens of buttons.

"Mr. Hughes," the voice came back over the speaker, "Lisa's here."

"Send her in. As I was saying, Grant, you'd get to see a lot about the inner workings of a big—"

His father kept talking as the door opened and the woman who was apparently Lisa came in, a blonde with wispy locks cut close to her head and earrings that brushed her shoulders.

"Hey, Mr. Hughes." She waved.

"Hey, Lisa." He winked at Grant, as if the "hey" were some kind of inside joke.

She carried a large, thin case on a strap over one shoulder and another case, a kit of some sort, in the other hand. Paying no attention to either of them, she proceeded around the side of the desk and began unsnapping the large case, hinging out the legs and setting up what Grant could see was some kind of portable table. She opened the other kit, displaying an elaborate set of scissors, bottles, and emery boards.

Pulling up a chair opposite his father, she unbuttoned his French cuffs, turned his sleeves back and dunked one hand into a creamy solution.

Grant's eyes traveled from the hand up his father's arm to his face and realized that his father was still talking.

"—thinking about a summer job with the firm. Maybe see what it would be like to work alongside his old man. Nash, Brakeman, Hughes & Hughes. Right, son?"

Grant nodded slightly, not wanting to, but not sure what else he could do. He had to break in, get this conversation back on track, or his time would be up and he would have accomplished nothing.

"Uh, Dad," he said, "actually, Dad, I came down here to talk to you for another reason . . . too." He added the "too" to soften it.

Lisa took the first hand out of the solution, dunked the second hand into it, patted the first hand dry, and started in on it with an emery board. The *swish swish* was loud and Grant raised his voice to talk over it.

"Actually, Dad, I came down today because I'm worried about Grandpa." There, at least he had started.

"Now, Grant, I know you're worried about your grandfather. But you don't need to be. His doctors are the best in the city. We're going to keep that old codger alive for a long time yet."

"Well, that's the thing, Dad." *Swish swish, swish swish.* "It's not the keeping him alive. I mean, I think we should think about it—"

Mmm mmm mmm.

His father took the hand that had been soaking out of the solution, picked up a pencil, and touched the button on the phone with the eraser end.

"Senator Boone, line one," the voice came over the speaker.

"Excuse me, Grant, but the Senator, you know," he said, pushing another button with the eraser, then plopping his hand back into the dish. "Bob! When are we going to get in that last set of tennis you owe me?"

He was so smooth with the sports BS. Not hitting things hard, head on, like Grant was trying to do. How did a person get to be so smooth?

While his father talked, Grant watched Lisa, still swish swishing the emery board. Her eyes darted up at Grant as she worked. They had a knowing look.

"Sorry for the interruption, Son. Now you were saying, about your grandfather. You're worried."

"Well, I'm worried, but not exactly for the reason you think I'm worried—"

Mmm mmm mmm.

His father picked his hand out of the solution again while Lisa filed away on the other.

"John Wiggins, line three, sir."

He punched line three. "Squire Wiggins, when are we going to get in that eighteen holes you promised me?"

The exact same routine. Man talk. Club talk. Lisa was more interesting than the phone call. She wiped the slick solution off the second hand and started in again with the emery board.

"Sorry, Grant. John Wiggins. President of Go

Chemical, you know. One of the firm's biggest clients. Anyway, you were saying, about your grandfather, go ahead. I'm listening."

Swish swish. Swish swish. "Yes. About Grandpa." Grant took a big breath. "And the life supports. I don't think you should put him on them—"

The door was opening behind him, over his last line, and he saw his father's eyes turn up to it. Grant looked back over his shoulder to see a secretary standing there.

"I know you're not expecting another call, but it's Judge Emerson. I thought I should warn you before you picked up. He's coming in on line four."

Grant turned back around to face his father, determined to go on. "—Dad, the machines, we should talk about it—"

His father took both hands away from Lisa, stopped Grant by signaling time out, then picked up the receiver. It was the first time Grant had seen him actually pick up the receiver. The other calls he had just handled over the speaker phone.

"Judge Emerson, Bill Hughes. What can I do for you, Your Honor? . . . Absolutely at your convenience, Your Honor . . . Twenty minutes is fine . . . Certainly, sir."

He punched another button and spoke briskly. "Evelyn. Emerson wants us up there in twenty minutes. Other side's already on their way. Sounds like a big pow-wow over the jury instructions. Get Morrison, he drafted them, the pleadings files, the research files for the instructions, and meet me at the elevators at"— he looked at his watch—"4:50. I have 4:40."

He hung up and looked at Lisa. "Can you finish me in two minutes?"

She nodded and speeded up the *swish swish*.

"Well, Grant, as you can see, I've got to cut this short. Judge Emerson is our judge for this case we're trying tomorrow. I've got to be in his chambers in twenty minutes and it takes ten to walk over. Now, you're welcome to come with us. It would be a real education for a young man who's interested in the law. And I could introduce you to Judge Emerson. I'd be proud to, in fact."

No. He shouldn't encourage his father in that line of thinking. "Think I'll pass."

"Well, suit yourself. And about this Grandpa business. Don't think I didn't hear you. That we need to think about it. Talk about it. But we don't, Son. It's all taken care of. I called the Home just today."

A lump formed in Grant's throat.

"Gave them the okay to do whatever they wanted. Hydration. Respirator. The works. So there's nothing to think about. Nothing to discuss. It's a done deal."

Grant's mouth went dry. As dry as Lisa's cotton balls.

"And you shouldn't be worrying about it. You should have your head on swim team and grades and that run for class president next—"

"Dad, Dad," Grant interrupted. "Are you saying they've already put him on? The machines?" His voice quavered as he struggled to keep his rising emotions—whether anger or fear he wasn't sure—under control.

"What? Already what?" His father had closed the matter, easy as closing a file, and moved on to the next item on his agenda.

"Already put him on the machines?" Grant planted his palms on the desk and leaned across. He could feel his body, moved by the adrenaline suddenly racing through him, rise several inches out of the chair. "Have they?" It was almost a shout, a desperate shout. "Have they?"

His father turned and looked at him—really *looked* at him, frozen there with his palms on the desk—and an odd look came over his father's face. A look Grant couldn't remember seeing there before. Was it surprise? As if he had just noticed Grant and was trying to remember why he was here? Bewilderment, because he had not the remotest idea what had brought on this outburst? Concern? Yes, that's what it was. His father was concerned about whatever it was that had Grant this worked up. He was going to ask Grant what was wrong, tell him they could talk about it.

But just then his father's eyes darted down and back. Grant didn't need to follow them to know where they had gone. Grant had lost to his father's wristwatch.

"Have they what? Put him on the machines? Well, Son, I'm not sure." It was his usual moving-matters-along voice.

So. He wasn't going to acknowledge the confrontation. Just smooth the moment over. Pretend it didn't happen. Sure. That would be the fastest way of dealing with it.

Grant could feel the tap of adrenaline turn off. His body sank slowly back into the chair as his father finished up with him.

"Just said they would put him on when they needed to, that's all." Then he turned to Lisa. "I can only give you one more minute, Lisa. Then I've got to run."

"I've just about got it, Mr. Hughes," she said, picking up a lambswool buffing cloth.

The secretary reappeared, set his father's briefcase down by the door, then took his suit coat off the coat tree. She held the jacket open for him, waiting, while Lisa turned his sleeves down and threaded his cufflinks through.

"Thanks, Lisa. Thanks, Carolyn. Carolyn, get Lisa a twenty." He stood up and let Carolyn put the jacket on him.

"I really enjoyed our visit, Son, and I want you to feel free to come back any time. Now think about that summer position, and I'll see you—well, maybe not tonight, because I'll be down here late, with the trial starting tomorrow and all—but, I'll see you."

Grant sat still, watching Lisa pack her supplies, snapping the table back into the flat travel case. And then she was gone, too.

Putting his forehead down on the polished tabletop in front of him, he noticed the glass of melting ice, still wedged between his knees. A few surviving pieces swam in the brown water. Melted. Diluted. Almost gone. It was just how he felt.

There was something about walking. The stride. The

rhythm. The next foot always appeared there, in front of the last one. The new leaves were out and the sycamores—planted by the bankers and oil barons who built this neighborhood—canopied the street, forming a cool, green passageway. They whispered to him as he walked home from his father's office.

"Grant, child, what is it worth you calling me away from my people?"

"I had to talk to you, Belle. I had to know."

"What's to know?"

"Is he on the machines?"

"Naw. Not yet. But it's coming. Your daddy talked to them today and we just have to get the D.O.—doctor's orders. That won't take long. Doubt he goes much longer by himself."

They exchanged silences over the phone wires.

"So how is he?"

"He's slipping, child. Sometimes he goes fifteen seconds without taking a breath. I know 'cause I just was in there and I've been counting it out. Hard to stand there and not count it out, if you know what I mean. Now, child, I'm goin' back to my people. But I want to tell you one thing. I know it like I know my own faith."

Grant waited for her to finish.

"Deuteronomy 33:12. 'The beloved of the Lord rest secure in Him.'"

That night, Grant sat at his desk, resting his forearms on the front edge to steady his hands. With a single-edged razor blade he sliced a red and yellow capsule in half over Grandpa's letter. After every three or four capsules, he tilted the paper into the mouth of a black plastic film container and tapped the powdery pile down the angle.

It had been spring break, when his family went skiing, that he had discovered the pills. Seeing his father pop the capsules before bed, he had asked if he was sick. It had started a fight. His mom said his dad had a problem if he was taking them even on vacation. "Not a big deal," his dad had said. "A normal thing, a *routine* thing," he had said, quoting his doctor. "Considering the stress I'm under."

One morning after they got home Grant went quietly down to his father's closet. He knew the Dopp kit would be there, always packed, on the shelf over the color wheel of neatly stacked sweaters. He took, *stole*, the orange plastic bottle and locked it away in the ivory drawer. Never heard a thing about it, not that he would have. Probably his father figured he had left the bottle sitting on a marble counter in some Hyatt.

At the time, stealing the pills had been just to be ready. In case. The way Randi described the quick shift of the relay baton in your hand. "Do it fast. As soon as you get the stick, and way before you're up to the next runner." That was all. At the time.

Grant counted the broken plastic skins as he gathered them up, then carried them into the bathroom on the letter and sprinkled them into the water. Standing there—watching the colored bits swirl around and down and out of sight—other bits and pieces came to him.

Avery: "I was afraid you were gonna miss your woo." "My what?" "Your woo. W-O-O. Window Of Opportunity."

Harland, the student nurse: "Glad to see there's a nice kid like you to look after him."

Coach: "Even good things can have bad consequences."

His mother: "Apply the law." Odd, how irrelevant the law part of it seemed to him now. That was the least of it.

Belle: "'I was hungry and you gave me food. I was thirsty and you gave me drink. I was sick and you looked after me.'"

His father, the first trip up to Grant's room: "You can get away with a lot if people trust you."

Grant's own voice: "Grandpa asked me for help . . . once."

His father's answer, the second trip up: "All I can say is, I hope you were quick about it. He must have been desperate."

The last of the bits disappeared.

Grant buried the loaded film container under his books, in the very bottom of his backpack. From now on he had better keep it with him.

13

The next four weeks were an exhausting roller-coaster ride. Not the modern kind of roller-coaster, smooth and sleek. The old-fashioned kind, on a rickety wooden trellis, that snapped your head back and banged your knees against the front of the tiny cart.

Grandpa had proved sturdier than anyone had predicted. He improved, then sank back, improved, then sank back. Each time he lost a little more color, was a little less responsive. But each time his body insisted on returning him, and so far the machines had not been connected.

It turned out that hydration and nutrition weren't his biggest problems. He was pretty good, still, at swallowing his liquid diet. It was his breathing—labored and erratic. The doctor had signed the standing order long ago, "Respirator when needed," but so far the machine had only been rolled in and posted at the head of Grandpa's bed, a sentinel on watch—knobs and dials for a face, hoses for arms. But Grant was keeping his own guard, one eye on the respirator for any sign of the first move.

Only twice since the visit to his father's office, the

walk home, the call to Belle—all of it a month ago—could Grant remember really letting down. Those were the two times he saw Randi.

Once he went with Avery's family to one of her track meets, and once she came to the city for the weekend. That Saturday he took her with him to visit Grandpa, telling him he had brought a friend. Grandpa heard the sound of her voice, so Grandpa knew—if he still heard, and Grant thought he did—that his friend was a girl. He wanted Grandpa to know that.

Other than that, the days were a blur, the scenery racing by too fast for him to see any of it.

As Grant crept to the top of what he somehow knew to be the final hill, he steeled himself, gripping the iron bar that locked him in. He was here by his own decision and there was no getting off. At least it would be over.

14

It was two o'clock in the morning and Grant stood in the shower, in the dark, letting the hot water pound down his back.

His head was splitting and algebra equations were swimming by in the steam in front of his eyes. It was no use. He couldn't remember any of them. What were these formulas for anyway? Was there one conceivable reason he would ever need to know any of them after noon tomorrow?

Tomorrow, Wednesday, was his last final; then he would be free. Not officially—school wasn't officially over until after the graduation ceremony Thursday morning. But for all practical purposes, tomorrow at noon was it.

Usually the last days of the school year were the sweetest—the anticipation, the counting down, the whole long summer stretching endlessly ahead. But he hadn't even thought about it.

He turned the water on hotter. Hot enough to turn his skin lobster red. Hot enough to hurt.

Grandpa was worse. Again.

These days, between Saturday visits, Grant regularly checked on Grandpa by calling Belle. This morning she had predicted to him that Grandpa would be on the respirator by the end of the week, unless there was some improvement. Which was always a chance, considering how things had gone.

But this time Grant didn't think so. The breathing was different, his lungs straining to squeeze each breath in and out. It was a thin ribbon of sound—less than a wheeze, almost a whistle. Like someone trapped deep in a mine shaft whistling to be found.

The sun shone in bright through the window over the desk at the end of the room. He had actually slept; that was a surprise. He felt good, refreshed. Primed for the test. More surprising.

As he had done every morning since he first put it there, Grant checked the film container in the bottom of his backpack, under his algebra book, and took off for school. It was early, because he wanted some time to review and because he was walking. He didn't ride his dirt bike anymore. His legs were too long, which was okay, 'cause he sorta felt too old for it, anyway.

Grant combed his fingers back through his hair. He had done it so many times his hands were oily. He wiped them off on his blue jeans so he could grip the pencil. Jotting in the last answer, he squared his scratch papers neatly under the test and looked up at the clock on the wall.

11:00. A whole hour early and he was finished. He should use the time to recheck his work—there were a couple of problems he wasn't that sure of—but he wasn't going to.

Banging a staple into the corner of the papers, he chucked them across the teacher's desk, smiled, and raised his fist in a silent "Yes!" to the envious eyes that followed him out of the room.

Grant gave his empty locker one final check. The hall was *so* quiet, and he was *so* free, he just had to slam it shut for good measure. Predictably—Grant waited for him—Crowder cracked his classroom door and peeked out, a turtle poking its head out of its shell. Who could have done such a thing in the middle of finals? Shooting him a thumbs-up, Grant slung his backpack, light now with only pencils, spiral rings, and the film container, over his shoulder. He was outta here.

It was called Our Lady's and it was Catholic and he had watched it pass by through the green-tinted window of the bus when he went to visit the Home every Saturday. That was about all he knew.

Creaking open one of the big wooden doors, he looked inside, letting the playful noises of uniformed children and bouncing rubber balls in with him. The sanctuary was light, with lots of windows, and decorated wedding-cake style, plaster cherubs and garlands trimming every inch. Not at all the somber gothic he had expected.

"Confessional hours 11:00 a.m. to 1:00 p.m., 5:00 p.m. to 7:00 p.m., Monday, Wednesday, Friday," he read on the sign on the little wooden closet standing in the niche. He hadn't known there were hours.

Was the priest in there already? How would he know? Or what if someone else were already inside?

Putting his ear to the back of the little structure—he couldn't help thinking it looked like a fancy out-house—he listened, as if for a heartbeat, but heard nothing. He looked quickly around to be sure no one was watching, but there were only two old women on pews near the front of the church. Taking a deep breath, he raised the black curtain and stepped inside.

It was a tiny space, completely filled by a small stool, a burning candle in a holder mounted to the wall, and the breathing, shifting sounds of the other human being which Grant now heard behind the wicker screen.

He sat down, looking straight ahead, and read the graffiti carved into the wood. "J.Q. + S.R. = Love." That one must be ancient. "The Father's a fuck-up." "Blue rules." "Call Candy for a hot lick."

He cleared his throat. "Sir," he whispered. "I don't know what to say."

"You say," the voice came back, low and old and patient, "'Father, forgive me, for I have sinned.'"

"Father, forgive me . . . for I have sinned," Grant repeated.

"Then you tell me how long it has been since your last confession."

"Father, it's been . . . fifteen years . . . since my last confession."

"Are you Catholic, my son?"

"No. Does it matter?"

"No. Not to me."

Grant slipped his hand down into his backpack, took out the film container, and wrapped his fingers around it.

"Is there something you came here to confess, my son? It's all right. You can say anything."

"I don't believe in God."

There was a moment of silence. "Is that what you came here to confess?"

"No."

"Go on."

"I pray every night for my grandfather, my grandpa, to die in his sleep."

"So you do believe in God."

"No. I don't. I just pray."

"Is that what you came here to confess?"

"No."

"Go on."

"I have pills in my pocket."

"And . . . "

"And my grandfather wants me to help him . . . to help him die."

Silence. Grant gripped the film container.

"Life is a gift, my son." In spite of what Grant had just confessed, the voice still sounded kind.

"I know."

"But it's not an unconditional gift. There are strings."

"Strings?"

"Such as, Be fruitful and multiply. Such as, Have dominion over the earth. Such as, Have no other gods before me and love thy neighbor as thyself. Such as, *You are not the one to decide when it is over. I, God, reserve that.* Life is a holy gift, my son. Only God gives it and only God takes it away."

"But I don't believe in God."

"You only think you don't."

Another silence.

"Your grandfather is sick?"

"Yes. Very sick. And suffering."

"Suffering can hold great power. Think of Our Lord on the cross. It is His suffering that saves us. Or think of someone else you know who has endured pain. Someone besides your grandfather."

The priest was waiting. Grant thought of Randi. "Okay."

"Now, I will tell you something about that person. That person is strong. That person is strong *because* of the suffering."

Grant didn't say anything, but he was thinking. He was thinking that it was true.

"You see, my son, suffering is part of God's plan. He didn't make a perfect world. He made a world with evil, Satan, the dark—call it whatever you want. And those things are part of the plan, too. Suffering *redeems* us."

"Redeems us from what?"

"From evil. From ourselves. From suffering."

"Suffering redeems us from suffering?"

"Yes."

"What else?" Grant asked.

"There are other reasons."

"Tell me. I want to hear them all. Every one that you can think of."

After another moment the priest went on. "Well, for one thing, it's rather egotistical, don't you think? For man to think he can make such a decision? Have such power? Over life itself? How foolish. How puffed up."

"What else?"

"Life is not a test you can race through and turn in early. He doesn't expect you to get a perfect score, but He does expect you to finish. If you turn the test in early, you have missed the point. You *fail*."

"What else?"

"What else do *you* say?"

Grant was quiet, thinking. Finally he spoke. "I say that I agree, life is a gift. But it's *his* gift, my grandfather's. Not yours. Not mine. Not the church's. He should be the one to say what he does with his gift.

"I say that my grandfather is very sick. I say that I don't think his suffering will make him stronger. He is too sick to be strong. His suffering is not making me stronger, either. It is making me sad.

"It probably is egotistical. But so is my grandfather. He is proud. If that's bad, I don't know. You said God gave man dominion. God made us higher. Maybe that's how we're higher, maybe we're *supposed* to make these decisions. Maybe.

"And, it might be safer not to turn the test in early. To look over your answers, use every second of your time. But sometimes the real test might be knowing that you've worked at it long enough. The real test might be knowing when it's time to quit."

They both sat quietly for a while; then Grant slipped the film container back down into the bottom of his backpack.

"Thank you, Father," he said, buckling the leather straps. "You might not think so, but you have helped me."

"You haven't told me—you are being cautious, I know, not to say too much—but I can see. Your mind's made up."

Grant said nothing.

"I have just one more question," the priest went on. "Can you live with yourself for the rest of your life if you do this thing of which you are thinking?"

"It's the same question I ask myself every night. Almost."

Now it was the priest's turn to wait.

"Every night"—the words caught in his throat, and Grant struggled to say them—"every night, I ask myself, can I live with myself for the rest of my life if I don't do it?"

Another silence. "In that case, before you leave, my son, there's one more thing I want to tell you. A story. Not a Bible story. Not a parable with a hidden meaning. A simple, true story, about myself and my family.

"I grew up in Kentucky. On a farm, out from town, with twelve sisters. I was the only boy, if you can believe that—number seven, right in the middle. Spoiled rotten, as you might guess. My mother died giving birth to my youngest sister, and so my mother's mother, my grandmother, lived in and took care of us.

"When I was twelve, my grandmother became ill. I don't know what it was, we just called it old age in those days. We made her a place on the pink silk divan in the parlor, and she lay there, watching us come and go around her. But she was in pain.

"One day the doctor rode out from town in his buggy and gave her a shot. Morphine, I suppose. And it helped. Because after the shot, she slept.

"Soon he began to come more often. Every other day, then every day. And my grandmother slept longer and longer. Finally she stopped waking up.

"Still the doctor kept coming, giving her the shot. Sometimes two shots, twice a day. And we watched her sleep harder and harder, there, on the pink divan. The only thing moving was her chest. Rising up and down. And each day it lifted less, until we had to kneel down and fix our eyes on it, to see if it moved at all.

"One day it didn't."

Grant was listening intently, poised on the edge of the little stool, his bag already over his shoulder. He waited a moment, to be sure the priest was finished, then spoke. "What are you saying? That the doctor killed her with the morphine?"

"I don't know."

"Put her to sleep?"

"I don't know."

"Was it a sin?"

"I don't know. Probably. Yes."

"Why did you tell me this?"

"I don't know. I just wanted you to hear it . . . And I want you to hear this, too. She was like my own mother. I loved her." The father's voice cracked. "And when it was over, I prayed, a prayer of thanksgiving."

As Grant pressed the heavy door open into the sunshine, he had the distinct feeling that someone was watching him. Looking back, he saw a figure in a black robe standing beside the confessional. He looked very old and very kind, as Grant had thought. The father's eyes caught the sun from the open door, and they flashed, wet and shining. Raising his arm toward Grant, he moved it slowly: up, down, side to side.

Was it a blessing or a prayer for his soul?

Grant spent that night in the tree house. He had never done it before, and he wasn't sure how he ended up there, but curled up in his sleeping bag he wasn't uncomfortable.

The stars were hidden, but he knew they were there, behind the vault of leaves. They put just enough light into the moonless night for Grant to see the branches twisting above him.

He saw the way they grew. Forking one way, then the other. That fork becoming its own branch and forking again. Left here, right there—was one way better or worse? Down to the tiniest twigs at the end of its reach, the tree was always branching, rebranching. Growing in a new direction. So many possible paths to the sky.

Grant remembered the summer nights he and Grandpa had slept out together, putting their sleeping bags down side by side on the hard, red earth. Just the two of them. *Goodnight, partner.*

Partners. That was the one thing he hadn't told the priest. Because the priest wouldn't have understood it. No one who hadn't burrowed in against the muscled chest that smelled like leather and fresh hay, no one who hadn't been rocked to sleep listening to the stories, would have understood it.

A partner shifts you when you've been riding drag at the rear of the herd, eating kicked-up dirt half the day. A partner ties a rope between his saddle horn and yours so if you get lost in the snow, at least you get lost together. A partner puts your horse down for you if he breaks a leg. A partner saws your own foot off if you're caught in a wolf trap.

Partners do for each other. Period.

15

The graduation ceremony was over and they were dropping him off on their way back downtown. As quietly as if its tires were made of velvet cushions, the black Mercedes rolled to a hushed stop in front of the Home. Grant got out, then rapped on his mother's window, which powered down.

"Why don't you guys come in with me?" he said, sticking his head in. "See Grandpa a minute. Tell him . . . hello."

"I'd like to, hon," his mother said, "but I've got a pre-trial docket starting in thirty minutes." She looked over at his father. "And I know your father needs to get back." She fingered Grant's bangs up and over. "How about we visit Grandpa this weekend? All of us together."

He nodded. It would come to pass, but not in the way she expected.

"Bye, hon," his mom yelled back through the open window, smiling and waving. "We're proud of you on your big day."

Looking around, Grant made a mental check list of the

things he would need. Water pitcher, full. Glass. Spoon. Straw. Leave the door to the hall open. No reason not to. They were used to him being here, feeding and taking care of him.

He opened the blinds so Grandpa could feel the warmth of the sun through the starched white sheets, then checked and rotated the plants under the window.

After raising the head of the bed to forty-five degrees, he lowered the railing and sat on the edge of the mattress, looking into his grandfather's face.

There were bruised, sunken-in circles under the eyes. Those were new. The white stubble of a beard poked bravely up.

He was awake, Grant could tell by the labored breathing—his chest didn't rattle as much when he slept—and there were little flickerings of almost-movements around his eyes and mouth.

Lifting Grandpa's hand, Grant remembered how hard it was to do even that, nine months ago. There were things he needed to tell him. And after a while he began.

"Guess what, Grandpa?" He spoke softly, stroking the pale, limp hand. "I graduated today, Grandpa. From middle school. Eighth grade. I thought you'd want to know."

Grant could feel the sinus cavities under his eyes begin to fill and thicken. "And guess what else? Mom *and* Dad came. Sat right smack in the middle of the very first row." He reached for a Kleenex and wiped under his nose. "And, of course, they clapped *way* too

hard when I got this award, the citizenship award"—
through sniffles, Grant was trying to sound cheerful—
"and, this is the worst part, while I'm up there, Mom
stands up, right in the middle of the front row, and
aims the video."

He pulled up another Kleenex. His eyes were filling with water, and he tried to hold the lids open wide
so they wouldn't overflow.

"It was totally embarrassing, and I told her so
after. She said, 'Don't you know, Grant, that's what
parents are for, to embarrass their children.'" He
blinked—couldn't not blink any longer—and a tear
overflowed the banks of his lids. Smearing it away
with the back of his sleeve, he struggled to go on.
"Why do parents always say that stuff? It's embarrassing.

"And you're not going to believe this." He tried to
smile through the tears, which were streaming now.
"You know Dad, always with his formal handshake
stuff. Well, after we'd gone through the 'Congratulations—Thank you, sir—Congratulations—Thank
you, sir' routine a zillion times, all of a sudden . . . no
warning at all . . . the guy reaches over and puts his
arms around me."

Grant breathed a shaky sigh. "I didn't really know
what to do. So, I put mine around him . . . I guess . . ."

A sob escaped, but he caught it halfway out and
swallowed it back down. "Anyway, we must have
hugged before. Probably lots, when I was little . . .
probably . . . but the thing is, I can't really remember
it. And I noticed, standing there, how . . . well . . .

how"—he choked on the words—"how *safe* it felt."

Grant sat on the edge of the bed, holding Grandpa's hand, and let nine months of tears come. Not that he could have kept them back any longer. It was as if his body knew what was ahead, and was emptying itself in preparation.

And then it was time.

After fumbling with the straps, Grant got his backpack open and fished out the black plastic film container.

In spite of his shaking hands, he managed to pour a small amount of water into the glass. Unsnapping the lid, he tapped the powder into the water.

He stirred, holding the glass up to the light, watching the liquid slosh higher and higher up the sides of the glass, as if rocked by an earthquake. He pressed the glass against his chest to quiet it, but felt it still rocked by his heart, pounding in his chest.

"You can do it, Hughes." It was Coach's voice, calling to him as he stood on the block shaking down "It's a matter of *not* telling yourself what to do. Te! your brain to shut up and let your body take over."

Grant took another deep breath, then bent over his grandfather's ear, so that the soft white h; growing out of the center brushed his nose.

"Grandpa," he whispered, "I've brought you ` drink. If you still want it."

Grandpa's eyes had stopped their restless i ments under his eyelids, and Grant felt that Gr heard. But he had to do more than hear. He *know.*

"Like the boy in the story, Grandpa." The story. It seemed so long ago that he had slipped the tape in and curled up in bed to listen to Grandpa whisper the story in his ear.

Grant zipped open the front pocket on his bag and fished around with his fingers, feeling for the hard smoothness of the stone. It was one of the stones Randi had found in the creek and given to him to skip on the pasture. He had saved this one, keeping it always with him.

Now, holding it out in the palm of his hand, he admired its even grayness. No markings. Completely ordinary. *Nothing lives long except the rocks.*

He kissed it, then quickly turned his grandfather's palm up and pressed the stone into it. He wrapped each of Grandpa's loose fingers around it, one by one, and then squeezed his own hand over his grandfather's—*hard*, trying to make Grandpa feel the stone, trying to make it *hurt*. Trying to feel the hard center for himself.

He took a deep breath and pushed himself on.

Slipping one arm behind his grandfather's shoulders, he raised his head up off the pillow. Holding the glass in his other hand, Grant pressed the straw to the parched lips.

"This is it, Grandpa."

Grandpa's lips clamped down over the straw and Grant watched the liquid climb. Grant felt panic beginning in his own insides, climbing and rising now in his own body, with the liquid. Was he sure of this? In a moment it would be too late not to be sure.

Just as the first of the solution disappeared between Grandpa's lips, Grandpa's eyes flew open. For one quick moment the glassy gaze was revealed— the eyes of a fish, caught and thrown up on the dock, staring right at Grant.

Grant dropped Grandpa's shoulders and jumped back, a cry of surprise rising up in his throat. He clamped his hands over his mouth to hold it down.

Thinking to look for the glass, he saw it, turned over on Grandpa's chest, the liquid flowing out of it and seeping into the thin gown. Then, as he watched, the glass began to roll toward the cliff of Grandpa's body, and the bigger cliff of the side of the bed.

Grant reached for it, he already knew, a moment too late.

The glass exploded on the tile.

Now people would come. They had heard and would come. Were coming already. He could hear someone down the hall. Grant looked around, panicked, checking for clues.

"Child, you're white as a ghost."

Belle.

"Mercy's sakes, it's only a spill. Happens all the time. Now go and get the broom to sweep up this glass. From the supply closet, down the hall, and I'll get him in something dry."

Grant didn't move. His eyes were glued to Grandpa's face. It looked the same. Eyes closed. Face quiet. Still, it had happened. Hadn't it?

He looked down at Grandpa's hand—the loose,

unfeeling fingers that he had arranged around the stone. They were curled in a tight fist. Grandpa was holding the stone on his own! He felt it. He *knew*.

Grant pulled the sheet up over Grandpa's fist, hiding it from Belle's view. As he did it, he felt his body, like the chain on a bicycle, slip into gear.

"Thanks, Belle, but you've got enough to do. I'll just stay and change him," Grant said, taking her elbow and escorting her toward the door. "It's my mess and I ought to be the one to take care of it."

"Well, that's sure the truth, and it's not like I don't have plenty to be doing. Here—" She stopped at the linen closet, pulled out a folded gown, and handed it to Grant, who was still at her elbow. "Be sure and get him nice'n dry. We don't want him catching pneumonia."

Alone in the room again, Grant scraped the broken glass under the bed with the sole of his shoe. He would sweep it up later. Untying the strings of his grandfather's wet nightgown, he patted his chest dry with a towel and put a clean gown on. He had dressed his grandfather many times before, and the familiar motions calmed him.

Grandpa was quiet, but he was still clutching the stone. Was he gone again? Biding his time? Saving his energy?

"Grandpa?"

He was moving his mouth. Was he trying to speak? Grant bent down. He could see him straining, gathering all of his breath to say it.

"Now."

My God. Grandpa had spoken. His voice was even dustier than Grant had remembered it, but it was still recognizable as Grandpa's own.

"You want me to go ahead? With the drink? Now?"

His head moved—was it a nod? A fraction of a fraction of a nod? Grant wasn't sure.

"But, Grandpa, you're awake. You might get better."

This time the word came again, and Grant knew it would be his last—every last bit of air was spent on getting the one before it out, yet this one came from somewhere, somewhere that did not have it to give. Grant could hear the near-anger behind it.

"Now!"

There was more powder. Grant had prepared exactly twice the number of pills he would need, just in case. Not for *this* reason. He hadn't expected this. But as a backup dose, in case the first solution wasn't strong enough, which he knew from his reading sometimes happened.

He pulled the container with the remaining half of the powder out of his backpack.

But the glass was broken. What could Grandpa drink from?

Fishing with his hand in the bottom of the backpack, Grant brought out his great-great-grandfather's tin trail cup.

Quickly he transferred his keys and change to his pocket, then mixed the new solution. This time he noticed his heart wasn't pounding, his hands weren't shaking. Calmly, he tinked the spoon dry on the edge of the cup.

"Now is a good time, Grandpa."

Grant put the cup in Grandpa's free hand—the hand that wasn't gripping the stone—and wrapped his grandfather's fingers around the cool metal, like a beggar's holding a tin cup. Then, for the first time in the nine months that he had been coming here, he felt it. Life! Fragile, but there, running in Grandpa's fingers as he held on to the cup, like sap running through the trees in winter. Astonished, Grant pulled his own hand away.

Grandpa held the cup on his own.

It was an act of sheer will. And of absolute love, Grant knew. Grandpa was holding the cup to save Grant from holding it.

But could he drink from it? Where was the straw? Maybe it had rolled under the bed when the glass fell. Or maybe Belle had thrown it away.

Before Grant could solve the problem, Grandpa, eyes closed, brought the cup slowly to his lips.

Grant hovered over Grandpa's face, breathing the same air in that Grandpa breathed out. As Grandpa drank, one belated tear slipped down Grant's cheek and into the solution, losing its separate identity with a plunk.

Grant packed the trail cup and film container back in the bottom of the backpack.

Then he slipped off his shoes and got into the bed, leaning Grandpa's head on his chest. He stroked the fine, white hair. It was the way Grandpa used to hold him in the rocking chair on the creaking front porch.

"I love you, Grandpa. And I miss you. I've been missing you for the last nine months. But I miss you most right now."

In only a minute or two he was asleep. Grant knew because the breathing stopped its rattling. Grant kissed the top of his head goodnight.

Another twenty minutes and the ever-present whistle of air that had accompanied his breathing for the last few days—the whistle of the trapped coal miners—stopped, too. Had they been found, or did their air just run out?

After that, the old air—ancient air, air that had been in Grandpa's body, deep down in his lungs, deep down in his gut, since who knew when—seeped out.

And it was over.

16

Standing with his parents on the cargo dock at the airport, Grant watched the mortuary staff—in black suits, even for this work—prepare the body for shipping, encased in its many layers of coffin, bubble wrap, fiberglass and cardboard. It looked like a refrigerator box. At the last moment, just as the workers in the bright orange coveralls were taking it away, Grant had asked if he could walk out with it.

"We're really not supposed to let you do that," said the young Hispanic man with black eyes just like Grant's, looking straight at him. "But I can't see as it'd hurt. Just one of you, though. Which one's the designated escort?"

"I am."

Grant's hand fell lightly on the cardboard and the stamped-on words HUMAN REMAINS as he walked beside the cart, out onto the tarmac, his parents watching from behind.

The plane's roar seemed fitting. It was a hot, windy day, and the sun reflected off the crystals in the cement and stabbed him in the eyes. Why did the scene feel familiar? Was it the same way the snow had blinded Grandpa Chaps's eyes, watching Fox Band carry Wandering Shadow's body away?

There were a couple of other items being loaded at this dock, not the regular dock, and the workers in the bright orange coveralls loaded those crates first.

Then the men motioned to him. Grant quickly pressed his fingers to the cardboard one last time and stepped aside. They shifted the box onto the lift and Grant stood, as if at attention, watching the body's slow ascent.

The plane moved under him, beginning its slow roll backward from the gate.

Sitting at the window, Grant looked out at the diminishing terminal, the windblown landscape. There was one cloud in the sky, and it must have dropped a quick sprinkle of rain, because the window was freckled with droplets of red Oklahoma dust, trapped inside the drops and then left behind by the evaporating water.

An aunt and uncle from Grandma's family would meet him in Portland, along with another mortuary staff. They had held the funeral here, and all they would do in Oregon was put him in the ground, so his parents weren't coming, though to Grant this was the most important part. Actually, he was glad it had turned out that way.

His version of what had happened was pretty much the truth. He told his parents he had gotten Grandpa water, which was when he dropped and broke the glass. Maybe the sound of the shattering glass had brought him to, he didn't know, but Grandpa had briefly opened his eyes and said something. Not too sure what. Surprised, Grant had given him more water, this time out of the trail cup because it was all he had handy, and even more surprising, Grandpa held it himself. He sat with him for a while, not wanting to leave, but Grandpa didn't do or say anything more and fell asleep. Later, Grant left to get a dustpan and broom to clean up the glass. When he came back, Grandpa was gone.

His mother had looked at him, hard, when he told it. Especially the part about the trail cup. But she didn't say anything.

"Maybe it was best this way," his dad had said, which Grant thought ironic, considering that his father had been the one who gave permission to connect the respirator; if it hadn't been for that, it might have come to pass "this way." But Grant realized it was easy for his father to say that now. Now it was something that had already happened, not something he would have to take time from his schedule to think about. In spite of this, Grant's anger toward his father had pretty much left him. Now, what he felt mostly toward his father was sorry.

When Grant told Belle about Grandpa coming to, she said, "It was his angel, child, come to wake him up and take him home." Said she had seen it lots of times, people reviving before they went.

Avery didn't say much. But that night they played basketball, even though it was Avery's graduation day too, and he could have been out celebrating. The thump of the ball on the cement echoed through the dark neighborhood until well after midnight.

Grant saw Randi in the yard of the church, with Avery's family, before the services. She came over and put her arms around him, even in front of his parents, and whispered in his ear. Of all of them, she was the only one it might be possible to tell. Not now. But someday.

And there were others at the funeral that it felt good to see. A few from the staff of the Home, including Harland, the student nurse, and Belle, of course. She was wearing a dove-gray hat and gloves that set off her cinnamon-colored skin. Grant had never seen her out of uniform. She was beautiful and dignified. Why had he never noticed that before?

There was a contingency from Nash, Brakeman & Hughes, including Evelyn and his father's secretary. And Vidella, their housekeeper. Even Coach was there. That was nice of him. And Dill, the handyman who still lived out on the ranch in a trailer. Grandpa's handwritten will had left the Rocking H in trust to Grant, and Grant had already made it clear that Dill had a home there as long as he wanted.

No one except Grant and the funeral parlor ever knew about the stone. Afterward, at the Home, Grant had folded Grandpa's arms over his chest, placing the hand with the stone underneath. Then he had pulled the sheet up over, taking his time arranging Grandpa and composing himself, before going to get Belle.

When the man came for the body, Grant tore a

sheet of paper out of his spiral ring, jotted a note, and tucked it inside Grandpa's gown. It said, "Dear Sir or Madam, Please ask whoever fixes the body to leave the object in my grandfather's hand. It's something that's just between the two of us, and I would like it to stay with him. Thank you, Grant Hughes. Grandson."

At the mortuary, where the body was on view, Grant had checked, lifting the cold, rubbery hands. They were so stiff they wouldn't raise much, but he could see the one underneath, fingers permanently curled, and he slipped his finger in to be sure. There was something hard in the center.

"Flight attendants, prepare for takeoff," the pilot commanded as the plane taxied into position.

Grant opened his backpack and took out a small leather book. Grandpa's diary. His mother had found it tucked inside the black Stetson when she was going through Grandpa's things. Grant had been saving it for now.

The engines revved under him.

The date at the top of the first page was more than sixteen years ago, before he was born. "I'm writing this to my Martha Jane," the diary began, "in case she ever wakes up. And, I guess too, just to keep myself company. Gets awful lonely out here these summer nights, sittin on the porch with the other rocker empty—"

Grant flipped through the pages. There were more of Grandpa Chaps's trail stories with Grandpa's own reminiscences spliced in between—taking a shower under a bucket with holes punched in it, sleeping on the ground with his boots under his head and, finding out later, a rattlesnake inside his boots. There were routine entries of daily ranch life—statistics regarding the stock, trouble with the pickup—and Grandpa's hopes for the new line of longhorns he had bred. There were original poems dedicated to "my girl" and recipes for soda biscuits cooked in a skillet on an open fire.

Grant looked up the date of his own birthday.

"My dearest Martha Jane, Our son had a son today—"

The plane started its roll down the runway.

"—and I'm burstin with the news. Bill called me from the hospital, bout the dadgum proudest man alive—"

Grant stopped reading and looked out the window, letting that last line echo in his head. The landscape was passing by at an ever-increasing speed, and it reminded him of his bike. The dirt bike. The bike he was too big for now. Maybe he would get the black mountain bike down from the hooks in the garage . . .

He went back to the diary. "Bill said he would bring me up to the hospital this evenin. But I couldn't wait, called a taxi, johnny on the spot. And I have to tell you, Martha Jane, he's the goddamned scrawniest package of lungs you ever saw. Looks bout like a just-dropped calf. And you know what? I'm goin to take him fishin and teach him to pluck the guitar and tell him all my stories that so far I've only told to you. All the things I never did with Bill cause I was always out fixin some goldurn fence."

So. Another piece to the puzzle. Maybe two pieces, to two puzzles.

"Me and this scrawny baby boy, we're gonna be good together—*partners*—I can feel it in my bones."

The plane was gaining speed.

"And Martha Jane, I already made his parents promise, as soon as he can leave the hospital, we're all gonna bring him out to see you, darlin. I'm gonna put him in your lap no matter how sick you are. Want you to feel him—the kick, the yawn, the curled-up fist—"

They were in the air.

"—the feel of brand-new life, hope itself, movin in your hands."

AUTHOR'S NOTE

I did not write this book to take a stand on the issue of assisted suicide. I wrote this book to tell a story. If, along the way, the story raises questions, that's a bonus. I have a firm belief that no matter what your thinking on any subject, fiction informs the debate in a way that mere facts never can.

But facts are important too. If you are brave enough to read accounts of actual assisted suicide, you will find that death rarely comes as easily as it did for Grandpa. I had Grandpa's frail body and stubborn-headedness to speed things along.

I should warn you: the nonfiction reading will make your stomach ache. At least I hope it will. No matter what position we take individually or as a society in dealing with this issue, if it ever doesn't make our stomachs ache, that's when we will really be in trouble.

B.S.G.
Oklahoma City
April 1996

169